Beowulf

J. Lesslie Hall

About the Author

J. Lesslie Hall

John Lesslie Hall (March 2, 1856 – February 23, 1928), also known as J. Lesslie Hall, was an American literary scholar and poet known for his translation of Beowulf.

Born in Richmond, Virginia, the son of Jacob Hall, Jr., Hall attended Randolph-Macon College and received a PhD from Johns Hopkins University. He taught English history and literature at the College of William and Mary from 1888 to 1928 (becoming head of the English department and dean of the faculty, and receiving an honorary LLD in 1921); he "was one of the original members of the faculty which reopened the college in 1888." He was also concerned with the history of his native Virginia; he frequently spoke at Jamestown and "compared Jamestown's Great Charter of 1618[clarification needed] and the assembly of 1619 with the Magna Charta at Runnymede."

In 1889 he married Margaret Fenwick Farland, of Tappahannock, Virginia. Their children were Channing Moore Hall, John L. Hall Jr., Joseph Farland Hall, and Sarah Moore Hall.

Beowulf

THE LIFE AND DEATH OF SCYLD.

The famous race of Spear-Danes.

Lo! the Spear-Danes' glory through splendid achievements

The folk-kings' former fame we have heard of,

How princes displayed then their prowess-in-battle.

Scyld, their mighty king, in honor of whom they are often called Scyldings. He is the great-grandfather of Hrothgar, so prominent in the poem.

Oft Scyld the Scefing from scathers in numbers

From many a people their mead-benches tore.

Since first he found him friendless and wretched,

The earl had had terror: comfort he got for it,

Waxed 'neath the welkin, world-honor gained,

Till all his neighbors o'er sea were compelled to

WAIT!

This book comes with an <u>Epic Bundle</u> of

8 FREE Audiobooks

10

Bow to his bidding and bring him their tribute:

An excellent atheling! After was borne him

A son is born to him, who receives the name of Beowulf—a name afterwards made so famous by the hero of the poem.

A son and heir, young in his dwelling,

Whom God-Father sent to solace the people.

He had marked the misery malice had caused them,

15

1That reaved of their rulers they wretched had erstwhile2

Long been afflicted. The Lord, in requital,

Wielder of Glory, with world-honor blessed him.

Famed was Beowulf, far spread the glory

Of Scyld's great son in the lands of the Danemen.

[2]The ideal Teutonic king lavishes gifts on his vassals.20

So the carle that is young, by kindnesses rendered

The friends of his father, with fees in abundance

Must be able to earn that when age approacheth

Eager companions aid him requitingly,

When war assaults him serve him as liegemen:

25

By praise-worthy actions must honor be got

'Mong all of the races. At the hour that was fated

Scyld dies at the hour appointed by Fate.

Scyld then departed to the All-Father's keeping

Warlike to wend him; away then they bare him

To the flood of the current, his fond-loving comrades,

30

As himself he had bidden, while the friend of the Scyldings

Word-sway wielded, and the well-lovèd land-prince

Long did rule them.3 The ring-stemmèd vessel,

Bark of the atheling, lay there at anchor,

Icy in glimmer and eager for sailing;

By his own request, his body is laid on a vessel and wafted seaward.35

The belovèd leader laid they down there,

Giver of rings, on the breast of the vessel,

The famed by the mainmast. A many of jewels,

Of fretted embossings, from far-lands brought over,

Was placed near at hand then; and heard I not ever

40

That a folk ever furnished a float more superbly

With weapons of warfare, weeds for the battle,

Bills and burnies; on his bosom sparkled

Many a jewel that with him must travel

On the flush of the flood afar on the current.

45

And favors no fewer they furnished him soothly,

Excellent folk-gems, than others had given him

He leaves Daneland on the breast of a bark.

Who when first he was born outward did send him

Lone on the main, the merest of infants:

And a gold-fashioned standard they stretched under heaven

[3]50

High o'er his head, let the holm-currents bear him,

Seaward consigned him: sad was their spirit,

Their mood very mournful. Men are not able

No one knows whither the boat drifted.

Soothly to tell us, they in halls who reside,4

Heroes under heaven, to what haven he hied.

[1] For the 'Þæt' of verse 15, Sievers suggests 'Þá' (= which). If this be accepted, the sentence 'He had ... afflicted' will read: He (i.e. God) had perceived the

malice-caused sorrow which they, lordless, had formerly long endured.

[2] For 'aldor-léase' (15) Gr. suggested 'aldor-ceare': He perceived their distress, that they formerly had suffered life-sorrow a long while.

[3] A very difficult passage. 'Áhte' (31) has no object. H. supplies 'geweald' from the context; and our translation is based upon this assumption, though it is far from satisfactory. Kl. suggests 'lændagas' for 'lange': And the beloved land-prince enjoyed (had) his transitory days (i.e. lived). B. suggests a dislocation; but this is a dangerous doctrine, pushed rather far by that eminent scholar.

[4] The reading of the H.-So. text has been quite closely followed; but some eminent scholars read 'séle-rædenne' for 'sele-rædende.' If that be adopted, the passage will read: Men cannot tell us, indeed, the order of Fate, etc. 'Sele-rædende' has two things to support it: (1) v. 1347; (2) it affords a parallel to 'men' in v. 50.

II.

SCYLD'S SUCCESSORS.—HROTHGAR'S GREAT MEAD-HALL.

Beowulf succeeds his father Scyld

In the boroughs then Beowulf, bairn of the Scyldings,

Belovèd land-prince, for long-lasting season

Was famed mid the folk (his father departed,

The prince from his dwelling), till afterward sprang

5

Great-minded Healfdene; the Danes in his lifetime

He graciously governed, grim-mooded, agèd.

Healfdene's birth.

Four bairns of his body born in succession

Woke in the world, war-troopers' leader

Heorogar, Hrothgar, and Halga the good;

10

Heard I that Elan was Ongentheow's consort,

He has three sons—one of them, Hrothgar—and a daughter named Elan. Hrothgar becomes a mighty king.

The well-beloved bedmate of the War-Scylfing leader.

Then glory in battle to Hrothgar was given,

Waxing of war-fame, that willingly kinsmen

Obeyed his bidding, till the boys grew to manhood,

15

A numerous band. It burned in his spirit

To urge his folk to found a great building,

A mead-hall grander than men of the era

He is eager to build a great hall in which he may feast his retainers

Ever had heard of, and in it to share

With young and old all of the blessings

20

The Lord had allowed him, save life and retainers.

Then the work I find afar was assigned

[4]

To many races in middle-earth's regions,

To adorn the great folk-hall. In due time it happened

Early 'mong men, that 'twas finished entirely,

25

The greatest of hall-buildings; Heorot he named it

The hall is completed, and is called Heort, or Heorot.

Who wide-reaching word-sway wielded 'mong earlmen.

His promise he brake not, rings he lavished,

Treasure at banquet. Towered the hall up

High and horn-crested, huge between antlers:

30

It battle-waves bided, the blasting fire-demon;

Ere long then from hottest hatred must sword-wrath

Arise for a woman's husband and father.

Then the mighty war-spirit1 endured for a season,

The Monster Grendel is madly envious of the Danemen's joy.

Bore it bitterly, he who bided in darkness,

35

That light-hearted laughter loud in the building

Greeted him daily; there was dulcet harp-music,

Clear song of the singer. He said that was able

[The course of the story is interrupted by a short reference to some old account of the creation.]

To tell from of old earthmen's beginnings,

That Father Almighty earth had created,

40

The winsome wold that the water encircleth,

Set exultingly the sun's and the moon's beams

To lavish their lustre on land-folk and races,

And earth He embellished in all her regions

With limbs and leaves; life He bestowed too

45

On all the kindreds that live under heaven.

The glee of the warriors is overcast by a horrible dread.

So blessed with abundance, brimming with joyance,

The warriors abided, till a certain one gan to

Dog them with deeds of direfullest malice,

A foe in the hall-building: this horrible stranger2

50

Was Grendel entitled, the march-stepper famous

Who3 dwelt in the moor-fens, the marsh and the fastness;

The wan-mooded being abode for a season

[5]

In the land of the giants, when the Lord and Creator

Had banned him and branded. For that bitter murder,

55

The killing of Abel, all-ruling Father

Cain is referred to as a progenitor of Grendel, and of monsters in general.

The kindred of Cain crushed with His vengeance;

In the feud He rejoiced not, but far away drove him

From kindred and kind, that crime to atone for,

Meter of Justice. Thence ill-favored creatures,

60

Elves and giants, monsters of ocean,

Came into being, and the giants that longtime

Grappled with God; He gave them requital.

[1] R. and t. B. prefer 'ellor-gæst' to 'ellen-gæst' (86): Then the stranger from afar endured, etc.

[2] Some authorities would translate 'demon' instead of 'stranger.'

[3] Some authorities arrange differently, and render: Who dwelt in the moor-fens, the marsh and the fastness, the land of the giant-race.

III.

GRENDEL THE MURDERER.

Grendel attacks the sleeping heroes

When the sun was sunken, he set out to visit

The lofty hall-building, how the Ring-Danes had used it

For beds and benches when the banquet was over.

Then he found there reposing many a noble

5

Asleep after supper; sorrow the heroes,1

Misery knew not. The monster of evil

Greedy and cruel tarried but little,

He drags off thirty of them, and devours them

Fell and frantic, and forced from their slumbers

Thirty of thanemen; thence he departed

10

Leaping and laughing, his lair to return to,

With surfeit of slaughter sallying homeward.

In the dusk of the dawning, as the day was just breaking,

Was Grendel's prowess revealed to the warriors:

A cry of agony goes up, when Grendel's horrible deed is fully realized.

Then, his meal-taking finished, a moan was uplifted,

15

Morning-cry mighty. The man-ruler famous,

The long-worthy atheling, sat very woful,

Suffered great sorrow, sighed for his liegemen,

[6]

When they had seen the track of the hateful pursuer,

The spirit accursèd: too crushing that sorrow,

The monster returns the next night.20

Too loathsome and lasting. Not longer he tarried,

But one night after continued his slaughter

Shameless and shocking, shrinking but little

From malice and murder; they mastered him fully.

He was easy to find then who otherwhere looked for

25

A pleasanter place of repose in the lodges,

A bed in the bowers. Then was brought to his notice

Told him truly by token apparent

The hall-thane's hatred: he held himself after

Further and faster who the foeman did baffle.

30

2So ruled he and strongly strove against justice

Lone against all men, till empty uptowered

King Hrothgar's agony and suspense last twelve years.

The choicest of houses. Long was the season:

Twelve-winters' time torture suffered

The friend of the Scyldings, every affliction,

35

Endless agony; hence it after3 became

Certainly known to the children of men

Sadly in measures, that long against Hrothgar

Grendel struggled:—his grudges he cherished,

Murderous malice, many a winter,

40

Strife unremitting, and peacefully wished he

4Life-woe to lift from no liegeman at all of

The men of the Dane-folk, for money to settle,

No counsellor needed count for a moment

[7]

On handsome amends at the hands of the murderer;

Grendel is unremitting in his persecutions.45

The monster of evil fiercely did harass,

16

The ill-planning death-shade, both elder and younger,

Trapping and tricking them. He trod every night then

The mist-covered moor-fens; men do not know where

Witches and wizards wander and ramble.

50

So the foe of mankind many of evils

Grievous injuries, often accomplished,

Horrible hermit; Heort he frequented,

Gem-bedecked palace, when night-shades had fallen

God is against the monster.

(Since God did oppose him, not the throne could he touch,5

55

The light-flashing jewel, love of Him knew not).

'Twas a fearful affliction to the friend of the Scyldings

The king and his council deliberate in vain.

Soul-crushing sorrow. Not seldom in private

Sat the king in his council; conference held they

What the braves should determine 'gainst terrors unlooked for.

They invoke the aid of their gods.60

At the shrines of their idols often they promised

Gifts and offerings, earnestly prayed they

The devil from hell would help them to lighten

Their people's oppression. Such practice they used then,

Hope of the heathen; hell they remembered

65

In innermost spirit, God they knew not,

The true God they do not know.

Judge of their actions, All-wielding Ruler,

No praise could they give the Guardian of Heaven,

The Wielder of Glory. Woe will be his who

Through furious hatred his spirit shall drive to

70

The clutch of the fire, no comfort shall look for,

Wax no wiser; well for the man who,

Living his life-days, his Lord may face

And find defence in his Father's embrace!

[1] The translation is based on 'weras,' adopted by H.-So.—K. and Th. read 'wera' and, arranging differently, render 119(2)-120: They knew not sorrow, the wretchedness of man, aught of misfortune.—For 'unhælo' (120) R. suggests 'unfælo': The uncanny creature, greedy and cruel, etc.

[2] S. rearranges and translates: So he ruled and struggled unjustly, one against all, till the noblest of buildings stood useless (it was a long while) twelve years' time: the friend of the Scyldings suffered distress, every woe, great sorrows, etc.

[3] For 'syððan,' B. suggests 'sárcwidum': Hence in mournful words it became well known, etc. Various other words beginning with 's' have been conjectured.

[4] The H.-So. glossary is very inconsistent in referring to this passage.—'Sibbe' (154), which H.-So. regards as an instr., B. takes as accus., obj. of 'wolde.' Putting a comma after Deniga, he renders: He did not desire peace with any of the Danes, nor did he wish to remove their life-woe, nor to settle for money.

[5] Of this difficult passage the following interpretations among others are given: (1) Though Grendel has frequented Heorot as a demon, he could not become ruler of the Danes, on account of his hostility to God. (2) Hrothgar was much grieved that Grendel had not appeared before his throne to receive presents. (3) He was not permitted to devastate the hall, on account of the Creator; i.e. God wished to make his visit fatal to him.—Ne ... wisse (169) W. renders: Nor had he any desire to do so; 'his' being obj. gen. = danach.

[8]

IV.

BEOWULF GOES TO HROTHGAR'S ASSISTANCE.

Hrothgar sees no way of escape from the persecutions of Grendel.

So Healfdene's kinsman constantly mused on

His long-lasting sorrow; the battle-thane clever

Was not anywise able evils to 'scape from:

Too crushing the sorrow that came to the people,

5

Loathsome and lasting the life-grinding torture,

Beowulf, the Geat, hero of the poem, hears of Hrothgar's sorrow, and resolves to go to his assistance.

Greatest of night-woes. So Higelac's liegeman,

Good amid Geatmen, of Grendel's achievements

Heard in his home:1 of heroes then living

He was stoutest and strongest, sturdy and noble.

10

He bade them prepare him a bark that was trusty;

He said he the war-king would seek o'er the ocean,

The folk-leader noble, since he needed retainers.

For the perilous project prudent companions

Chided him little, though loving him dearly;

15

They egged the brave atheling, augured him glory.

With fourteen carefully chosen companions, he sets out for Dane-land.

The excellent knight from the folk of the Geatmen

Had liegemen selected, likest to prove them

Trustworthy warriors; with fourteen companions

The vessel he looked for; a liegeman then showed them,

20

A sea-crafty man, the bounds of the country.

Fast the days fleeted; the float was a-water,

The craft by the cliff. Clomb to the prow then

Well-equipped warriors: the wave-currents twisted

The sea on the sand; soldiers then carried

25

On the breast of the vessel bright-shining jewels,

Handsome war-armor; heroes outshoved then,

Warmen the wood-ship, on its wished-for adventure.

[9]The vessel sails like a bird

The foamy-necked floater fanned by the breeze,

Likest a bird, glided the waters,

In twenty four hours they reach the shores of Hrothgar's dominions30

Till twenty and four hours thereafter

The twist-stemmed vessel had traveled such distance

That the sailing-men saw the sloping embankments,

The sea cliffs gleaming, precipitous mountains,

Nesses enormous: they were nearing the limits

35

At the end of the ocean.2 Up thence quickly

The men of the Weders clomb to the mainland,

Fastened their vessel (battle weeds rattled,

War burnies clattered), the Wielder they thanked

That the ways o'er the waters had waxen so gentle.

They are hailed by the Danish coast guard40

Then well from the cliff edge the guard of the Scyldings

Who the sea-cliffs should see to, saw o'er the gangway

Brave ones bearing beauteous targets,

Armor all ready, anxiously thought he,

Musing and wondering what men were approaching.

45

High on his horse then Hrothgar's retainer

Turned him to coastward, mightily brandished

His lance in his hands, questioned with boldness.

His challenge

"Who are ye men here, mail-covered warriors

Clad in your corslets, come thus a-driving

50

A high riding ship o'er the shoals of the waters,

3And hither 'neath helmets have hied o'er the ocean?

[10]

I have been strand-guard, standing as warden,

Lest enemies ever anywise ravage

Danish dominions with army of war-ships.

55

More boldly never have warriors ventured

Hither to come; of kinsmen's approval,

Word-leave of warriors, I ween that ye surely

He is struck by Beowulf's appearance.

Nothing have known. Never a greater one

Of earls o'er the earth have I had a sight of

60

Than is one of your number, a hero in armor;

No low-ranking fellow4 adorned with his weapons,

But launching them little, unless looks are deceiving,

And striking appearance. Ere ye pass on your journey

As treacherous spies to the land of the Scyldings

65

And farther fare, I fully must know now

What race ye belong to. Ye far-away dwellers,

Sea-faring sailors, my simple opinion

Hear ye and hearken: haste is most fitting

Plainly to tell me what place ye are come from."

[1] 'From hám' (194) is much disputed. One rendering is: Beowulf, being away from home, heard of Hrothgar's troubles, etc. Another, that adopted by S. and endorsed in the H.-So. notes, is: B. heard from his neighborhood (neighbors), i.e. in his home, etc. A third is: B., being at home, heard this as occurring away from home. The H.-So. glossary and notes conflict.

[2] 'Eoletes' (224) is marked with a (?) by H.-So.; our rendering simply follows his conjecture.—Other conjectures as to 'eolet' are: (1) voyage, (2) toil, labor, (3) hasty journey.

[3] The lacuna of the MS at this point has been supplied by various conjectures. The reading adopted by H.-So. has been rendered in the above translation. W., like H.-So., makes 'ic' the beginning of a new sentence, but, for 'helmas bæron,' he reads 'hringed stefnan.' This has the advantage of giving a parallel to 'brontne ceol' instead of a kenning for 'go.'—B puts the (?) after 'holmas', and begins a new sentence at the middle of the line. Translate: What warriors are ye, clad in armor, who have thus come bringing the foaming vessel over the water way, hither over the seas? For some time on the wall I have been coast guard, etc. S. endorses most of what B. says, but leaves out 'on the wall' in the last sentence. If W.'s 'hringed stefnan' be accepted, change line 51 above to, A ring-stemmed vessel hither o'ersea.

[4] 'Seld-guma' (249) is variously rendered: (1) housecarle; (2) home-stayer; (3) common man. Dr. H. Wood suggests a man-at-arms in another's house.

V.

THE GEATS REACH HEOROT.

Beowulf courteously replies.

The chief of the strangers rendered him answer,

War-troopers' leader, and word-treasure opened:

We are Geats.

"We are sprung from the lineage of the people of Geatland,

And Higelac's hearth-friends. To heroes unnumbered

My father Ecgtheow was well-known in his day.5

My father was known, a noble head-warrior

Ecgtheow titled; many a winter

He lived with the people, ere he passed on his journey,

Old from his dwelling; each of the counsellors

Widely mid world-folk well remembers him.

Our intentions towards King Hrothgar are of the kindest.10

We, kindly of spirit, the lord of thy people,

The son of King Healfdene, have come here to visit,

[11]

Folk-troop's defender: be free in thy counsels!

To the noble one bear we a weighty commission,

The helm of the Danemen; we shall hide, I ween,

Is it true that a monster is slaying Danish heroes?15

Naught of our message. Thou know'st if it happen,

As we soothly heard say, that some savage despoiler,

Some hidden pursuer, on nights that are murky

By deeds very direful 'mid the Danemen exhibits

Hatred unheard of, horrid destruction

20

And the falling of dead. From feelings least selfish

I can help your king to free himself from this horrible creature.

I am able to render counsel to Hrothgar,

How he, wise and worthy, may worst the destroyer,

If the anguish of sorrow should ever be lessened,1

Comfort come to him, and care-waves grow cooler,

Or ever hereafter he agony suffer

And troublous distress, while towereth upward

The handsomest of houses high on the summit."

The coast-guard reminds Beowulf that it is easier to say than to do.

Bestriding his stallion, the strand-watchman answered,

The doughty retainer: "The difference surely

30

'Twixt words and works, the warlike shield-bearer

Who judgeth wisely well shall determine.

This band, I hear, beareth no malice

I am satisfied of your good intentions, and shall lead you to the palace.

To the prince of the Scyldings. Pass ye then onward

With weapons and armor. I shall lead you in person;

35

To my war-trusty vassals command I shall issue

To keep from all injury your excellent vessel,

Your boat shall be well cared for during your stay here.

Your fresh-tarred craft, 'gainst every opposer

Close by the sea-shore, till the curved-neckèd bark shall

Waft back again the well-beloved hero

40

O'er the way of the water to Weder dominions.

He again compliments Beowulf.

To warrior so great 'twill be granted sure

In the storm of strife to stand secure."

Onward they fared then (the vessel lay quiet,

The broad-bosomed bark was bound by its cable,

[12]45

Firmly at anchor); the boar-signs glistened2

Bright on the visors vivid with gilding,

Blaze-hardened, brilliant; the boar acted warden.

The heroes hastened, hurried the liegemen,

The land is perhaps rolling.

Descended together, till they saw the great palace,

50

The well-fashioned wassail-hall wondrous and gleaming:

Heorot flashes on their view.

'Mid world-folk and kindreds that was widest reputed

Of halls under heaven which the hero abode in;

Its lustre enlightened lands without number.

Then the battle-brave hero showed them the glittering

55

Court of the bold ones, that they easily thither

Might fare on their journey; the aforementioned warrior

Turning his courser, quoth as he left them:

The coast-guard, having discharged his duty, bids them God-speed.

"'Tis time I were faring; Father Almighty

Grant you His grace, and give you to journey

60

Safe on your mission! To the sea I will get me

'Gainst hostile warriors as warden to stand."

[1] 'Edwendan' (280) B. takes to be the subs. 'edwenden' (cf. 1775); and 'bisigu' he takes as gen. sing., limiting 'edwenden': If reparation for sorrows is ever to come. This is supported by t.B.

[2] Combining the emendations of B. and t.B., we may read: The boar-images glistened ... brilliant, protected the life of the war-mooded man. They read 'ferh-wearde' (305) and 'gúðmódgum men' (306).

VI.

BEOWULF INTRODUCES HIMSELF AT THE PALACE.

The highway glistened with many-hued pebble,

A by-path led the liegemen together.

1Firm and hand-locked the war-burnie glistened,

The ring-sword radiant rang 'mid the armor

5

As the party was approaching the palace together

They set their arms and armor against the wall.

In warlike equipments. 'Gainst the wall of the building

Their wide-fashioned war-shields they weary did set then,

[13]

Battle-shields sturdy; benchward they turned then;

Their battle-sarks rattled, the gear of the heroes;

10

The lances stood up then, all in a cluster,

The arms of the seamen, ashen-shafts mounted

With edges of iron: the armor-clad troopers

A Danish hero asks them whence and why they are come.

Were decked with weapons. Then a proud-mooded hero

Asked of the champions questions of lineage:

15

"From what borders bear ye your battle-shields plated,

Gilded and gleaming, your gray-colored burnies,

Helmets with visors and heap of war-lances?—

To Hrothgar the king I am servant and liegeman.

'Mong folk from far-lands found I have never

He expresses no little admiration for the strangers.20

Men so many of mien more courageous.

I ween that from valor, nowise as outlaws,

But from greatness of soul ye sought for King Hrothgar."

Beowulf replies.

Then the strength-famous earlman answer rendered,

The proud-mooded Wederchief replied to his question,

We are Higelac's table-companions, and bear an important commission to your prince.25

Hardy 'neath helmet: "Higelac's mates are we;

Beowulf hight I. To the bairn of Healfdene,

The famous folk-leader, I freely will tell

To thy prince my commission, if pleasantly hearing

He'll grant we may greet him so gracious to all men."

30

Wulfgar replied then (he was prince of the Wendels,

His boldness of spirit was known unto many,

His prowess and prudence): "The prince of the Scyldings,

Wulfgar, the thane, says that he will go and ask Hrothgar whether he will see the strangers.

The friend-lord of Danemen, I will ask of thy journey,

The giver of rings, as thou urgest me do it,

35

The folk-chief famous, and inform thee early

What answer the good one mindeth to render me."

He turned then hurriedly where Hrothgar was sitting,

2Old and hoary, his earlmen attending him;

The strength-famous went till he stood at the shoulder

40

Of the lord of the Danemen, of courteous thanemen

The custom he minded. Wulfgar addressed then

His friendly liegelord: "Folk of the Geatmen

[14]He thereupon urges his liegelord to receive the visitors courteously.

O'er the way of the waters are wafted hither,

Faring from far-lands: the foremost in rank

WAIT!

This book comes with an <u>Epic Bundle</u> of

8 FREE Audiobooks

<u>https://gum.co/epic-8-audiobooks-bundle/secret-2016</u>

45

The battle-champions Beowulf title.

They make this petition: with thee, O my chieftain,

To be granted a conference; O gracious King Hrothgar,

Friendly answer refuse not to give them!

Hrothgar, too, is struck with Beowulf's appearance.

In war-trappings weeded worthy they seem

50

Of earls to be honored; sure the atheling is doughty

Who headed the heroes hitherward coming."

[1] Instead of the punctuation given by H.-So, S. proposed to insert a comma after 'scír' (322), and to take 'hring-íren' as meaning 'ring-mail' and as parallel with 'gúð-byrne.' The passage would then read: The firm and hand-locked war-burnie shone, bright ring-mail, rang 'mid the armor, etc.

[2] Gr. and others translate 'unhár' by 'bald'; old and bald.

VII.

HROTHGAR AND BEOWULF.

Hrothgar remembers Beowulf as a youth, and also remembers his father.

Hrothgar answered, helm of the Scyldings:

"I remember this man as the merest of striplings.

His father long dead now was Ecgtheow titled,

Him Hrethel the Geatman granted at home his

5

One only daughter; his battle-brave son

Is come but now, sought a trustworthy friend.

Seafaring sailors asserted it then,

Beowulf is reported to have the strength of thirty men.

Who valuable gift-gems of the Geatmen1 carried

As peace-offering thither, that he thirty men's grapple

10

Has in his hand, the hero-in-battle.

God hath sent him to our rescue.

The holy Creator usward sent him,

To West-Dane warriors, I ween, for to render

'Gainst Grendel's grimness gracious assistance:

I shall give to the good one gift-gems for courage.

15

Hasten to bid them hither to speed them,2

To see assembled this circle of kinsmen;

Tell them expressly they're welcome in sooth to

The men of the Danes." To the door of the building

[15]Wulfgar invites the strangers in.

Wulfgar went then, this word-message shouted:

20

"My victorious liegelord bade me to tell you,

The East-Danes' atheling, that your origin knows he,

And o'er wave-billows wafted ye welcome are hither,

Valiant of spirit. Ye straightway may enter

Clad in corslets, cased in your helmets,

25

To see King Hrothgar. Here let your battle-boards,

Wood-spears and war-shafts, await your conferring."

The mighty one rose then, with many a liegeman,

An excellent thane-group; some there did await them,

And as bid of the brave one the battle-gear guarded.

30

Together they hied them, while the hero did guide them,

'Neath Heorot's roof; the high-minded went then

Sturdy 'neath helmet till he stood in the building.

Beowulf spake (his burnie did glisten,

His armor seamed over by the art of the craftsman):

Beowulf salutes Hrothgar, and then proceeds to boast of his youthful achievements.35

"Hail thou, Hrothgar! I am Higelac's kinsman

And vassal forsooth; many a wonder

I dared as a stripling. The doings of Grendel,

In far-off fatherland I fully did know of:

Sea-farers tell us, this hall-building standeth,

40

Excellent edifice, empty and useless

To all the earlmen after evenlight's glimmer

'Neath heaven's bright hues hath hidden its glory.

This my earls then urged me, the most excellent of them,

Carles very clever, to come and assist thee,

45

Folk-leader Hrothgar; fully they knew of

His fight with the nickers.

The strength of my body. Themselves they beheld me

When I came from the contest, when covered with gore

Foes I escaped from, where five3 I had bound,

[16]

The giant-race wasted, in the waters destroying

50

The nickers by night, bore numberless sorrows,

The Weders avenged (woes had they suffered)

Enemies ravaged; alone now with Grendel

He intends to fight Grendel unaided.

I shall manage the matter, with the monster of evil,

The giant, decide it. Thee I would therefore

55

Beg of thy bounty, Bright-Danish chieftain,

Lord of the Scyldings, this single petition:

Not to refuse me, defender of warriors,

Friend-lord of folks, so far have I sought thee,

That I may unaided, my earlmen assisting me,

60

This brave-mooded war-band, purify Heorot.

I have heard on inquiry, the horrible creature

Since the monster uses no weapons,

From veriest rashness recks not for weapons;

I this do scorn then, so be Higelac gracious,

My liegelord belovèd, lenient of spirit,

65

To bear a blade or a broad-fashioned target,

A shield to the onset; only with hand-grip

I, too, shall disdain to use any.

The foe I must grapple, fight for my life then,

Foeman with foeman; he fain must rely on

The doom of the Lord whom death layeth hold of.

Should he crush me, he will eat my companions as he has eaten thy thanes.70

I ween he will wish, if he win in the struggle,

To eat in the war-hall earls of the Geat-folk,

Boldly to swallow4 them, as of yore he did often

The best of the Hrethmen! Thou needest not trouble

A head-watch to give me;5 he will have me dripping

[17]In case of my defeat, thou wilt not have the trouble of burying me.75

And dreary with gore, if death overtake me,6

Will bear me off bleeding, biting and mouthing me,

The hermit will eat me, heedless of pity,

Marking the moor-fens; no more wilt thou need then

Should I fall, send my armor to my lord, King Higelac.

Find me my food.7 If I fall in the battle,

80

Send to Higelac the armor that serveth

To shield my bosom, the best of equipments,

Richest of ring-mails; 'tis the relic of Hrethla,

Weird is supreme

The work of Wayland. Goes Weird as she must go!"

[1] Some render 'gif-sceattas' by 'tribute.'—'Géata' B. and Th. emended to 'Géatum.' If this be accepted, change 'of the Geatmen' to 'to the Geatmen.'

[2] If t.B.'s emendation of vv. 386, 387 be accepted, the two lines, 'Hasten … kinsmen' will read: Hasten thou, bid the throng of kinsmen go into the hall together.

[3] For 420 (b) and 421 (a), B. suggests: Þær ic (on) fifelgeban ýðde eotena cyn = where I in the ocean destroyed the eoten-race.—t.B. accepts B.'s "brilliant" 'fifelgeban,' omits 'on,' emends 'cyn' to 'hám,' arranging: Þær ic fifelgeban ýðde, eotena hám = where I desolated the ocean, the home of the eotens.—This would be better but for changing 'cyn' to 'hám.'—I suggest: Þær ic fifelgeband (cf. nhd. Bande) ýðde, eotena cyn = where I conquered the monster band, the race of the eotens. This makes no change except to read 'fifel' for 'fife.'

[4] 'Unforhte' (444) is much disputed.—H.-So. wavers between adj. and adv. Gr. and B. take it as an adv. modifying etan: Will eat the Geats fearlessly.—Kl. considers this reading absurd, and proposes 'anforhte' = timid.—Understanding 'unforhte' as an adj. has this advantage, viz. that it gives a parallel to 'Geátena leóde': but to take it as an adv. is more natural. Furthermore, to call the Geats 'brave' might, at this point, seem like an implied thrust at the Danes, so long helpless; while to call his own men 'timid' would be befouling his own nest.

[5] For 'head-watch,' cf. H.-So. notes and cf. v. 2910.—Th. translates: Thou wilt not need my head to hide (i.e., thou wilt have no occasion to bury me, as Grendel will devour me whole).—Simrock imagines a kind of dead-watch.—Dr. H. Wood suggests: Thou wilt not have to bury so much as my head (for Grendel will be a thorough undertaker),—grim humor.

40

[6] S. proposes a colon after 'nimeð' (l. 447). This would make no essential change in the translation.

[7] Owing to the vagueness of 'feorme' (451), this passage is variously translated. In our translation, H.-So.'s glossary has been quite closely followed. This agrees substantially with B.'s translation (P. and B. XII. 87). R. translates: Thou needst not take care longer as to the consumption of my dead body. 'Líc' is also a crux here, as it may mean living body or dead body.

VIII.

HROTHGAR AND BEOWULF.—Continued.

Hrothgar responds.

Hrothgar discoursed, helm of the Scyldings:

"To defend our folk and to furnish assistance,1

Thou soughtest us hither, good friend Beowulf.

Reminiscences of Beowulf's father, Ecgtheow.

The fiercest of feuds thy father engaged in,

5

Heatholaf killed he in hand-to-hand conflict

'Mid Wilfingish warriors; then the Wederish people

For fear of a feud were forced to disown him.

Thence flying he fled to the folk of the South-Danes,

[18]

The race of the Scyldings, o'er the roll of the waters;

41

10

I had lately begun then to govern the Danemen,

The hoard-seat of heroes held in my youth,

Rich in its jewels: dead was Heregar,

My kinsman and elder had earth-joys forsaken,

Healfdene his bairn. He was better than I am!

15

That feud thereafter for a fee I compounded;

O'er the weltering waters to the Wilfings I sent

Ornaments old; oaths did he swear me.

Hrothgar recounts to Beowulf the horrors of Grendel's persecutions.

It pains me in spirit to any to tell it,

What grief in Heorot Grendel hath caused me,

20

What horror unlooked-for, by hatred unceasing.

Waned is my war-band, wasted my hall-troop;

Weird hath offcast them to the clutches of Grendel.

God can easily hinder the scather

From deeds so direful. Oft drunken with beer

My thanes have made many boasts, but have not executed them.25

O'er the ale-vessel promised warriors in armor

They would willingly wait on the wassailing-benches

A grapple with Grendel, with grimmest of edges.

Then this mead-hall at morning with murder was reeking,

The building was bloody at breaking of daylight,

30

The bench-deals all flooded, dripping and bloodied,

The folk-hall was gory: I had fewer retainers,

Dear-beloved warriors, whom death had laid hold of.

Sit down to the feast, and give us comfort.

Sit at the feast now, thy intents unto heroes,2

Thy victor-fame show, as thy spirit doth urge thee!"

A bench is made ready for Beowulf and his party.35

For the men of the Geats then together assembled,

In the beer-hall blithesome a bench was made ready;

There warlike in spirit they went to be seated,

Proud and exultant. A liegeman did service,

[19]

Who a beaker embellished bore with decorum,

The gleeman sings40

And gleaming-drink poured. The gleeman sang whilom

The heroes all rejoice together.

Hearty in Heorot; there was heroes' rejoicing,

A numerous war-band of Weders and Danemen.

[1] B. and S. reject the reading given in H.-So., and suggested by Grtvg. B. suggests for 457-458:

wáere-ryhtum Þú, wine mín Béowulf,

and for ár-stafum úsic sóhtest.

This means: From the obligations of clientage, my friend Beowulf, and for assistance thou hast sought us.—This gives coherence to Hrothgar's opening remarks in VIII., and also introduces a new motive for Beowulf's coming to Hrothgar's aid.

[2] Sit now at the feast, and disclose thy purposes to the victorious heroes, as thy spirit urges.—Kl. reaches the above translation by erasing the comma after 'meoto' and reading 'sige-hrèðsecgum.'—There are other and bolder emendations and suggestions. Of these the boldest is to regard 'meoto' as a verb (imperative), and read 'on sæl': Think upon gayety, etc.—All the renderings are unsatisfactory, the one given in our translation involving a zeugma.

IX.

UNFERTH TAUNTS BEOWULF.

Unferth, a thane of Hrothgar, is jealous of Beowulf, and undertakes to twit him.

Unferth spoke up, Ecglaf his son,

Who sat at the feet of the lord of the Scyldings,

Opened the jousting (the journey1 of Beowulf,

Sea-farer doughty, gave sorrow to Unferth

5

And greatest chagrin, too, for granted he never

That any man else on earth should attain to,

Gain under heaven, more glory than he):

Did you take part in a swimming-match with Breca?

"Art thou that Beowulf with Breca did struggle,

On the wide sea-currents at swimming contended,

10

Where to humor your pride the ocean ye tried,

'Twas mere folly that actuated you both to risk your lives on the ocean.

From vainest vaunting adventured your bodies

In care of the waters? And no one was able

Nor lief nor loth one, in the least to dissuade you

Your difficult voyage; then ye ventured a-swimming,

15

Where your arms outstretching the streams ye did cover,

The mere-ways measured, mixing and stirring them,

Glided the ocean; angry the waves were,

With the weltering of winter. In the water's possession,

Ye toiled for a seven-night; he at swimming outdid thee,

20

In strength excelled thee. Then early at morning

On the Heathoremes' shore the holm-currents tossed him,

Sought he thenceward the home of his fathers,

Beloved of his liegemen, the land of the Brondings,

The peace-castle pleasant, where a people he wielded,

[20]25

Had borough and jewels. The pledge that he made thee

Breca outdid you entirely.

The son of Beanstan hath soothly accomplished.

Then I ween thou wilt find thee less fortunate issue,

Much more will Grendel outdo you, if you vie with him in prowess.

Though ever triumphant in onset of battle,

A grim grappling, if Grendel thou darest

30

For the space of a night near-by to wait for!"

Beowulf retaliates.

Beowulf answered, offspring of Ecgtheow:

"My good friend Unferth, sure freely and wildly,

O friend Unferth, you are fuddled with beer, and cannot talk coherently.

Thou fuddled with beer of Breca hast spoken,

Hast told of his journey! A fact I allege it,

35

That greater strength in the waters I had then,

Ills in the ocean, than any man else had.

We made agreement as the merest of striplings

Promised each other (both of us then were

We simply kept an engagement made in early life.

Younkers in years) that we yet would adventure

40

Out on the ocean; it all we accomplished.

While swimming the sea-floods, sword-blade unscabbarded

Boldly we brandished, our bodies expected

To shield from the sharks. He sure was unable

He could not excel me, and I would not excel him.

To swim on the waters further than I could,

45

More swift on the waves, nor would I from him go.

Then we two companions stayed in the ocean

After five days the currents separated us.

Five nights together, till the currents did part us,

The weltering waters, weathers the bleakest,

And nethermost night, and the north-wind whistled

50

Fierce in our faces; fell were the billows.

The mere fishes' mood was mightily ruffled:

And there against foemen my firm-knotted corslet,

Hand-jointed, hardy, help did afford me;

My battle-sark braided, brilliantly gilded,

A horrible sea-beast attacked me, but I slew him.55

Lay on my bosom. To the bottom then dragged me,

A hateful fiend-scather, seized me and held me,

Grim in his grapple: 'twas granted me, nathless,

To pierce the monster with the point of my weapon,

My obedient blade; battle offcarried

60

The mighty mere-creature by means of my hand-blow.

[1] It has been plausibly suggested that 'síð' (in 501 and in 353) means 'arrival.' If so, translate the bracket: (the arrival of Beowulf, the brave seafarer, was a source of great chagrin to Unferth, etc.).

[21]

X.

BEOWULF SILENCES UNFERTH.—GLEE IS HIGH.

"So ill-meaning enemies often did cause me

Sorrow the sorest. I served them, in quittance,

My dear sword always served me faithfully.

With my dear-lovèd sword, as in sooth it was fitting;

They missed the pleasure of feasting abundantly,

5

Ill-doers evil, of eating my body,

Of surrounding the banquet deep in the ocean;

But wounded with edges early at morning

They were stretched a-high on the strand of the ocean,

I put a stop to the outrages of the sea-monsters.

Put to sleep with the sword, that sea-going travelers

10

No longer thereafter were hindered from sailing

The foam-dashing currents. Came a light from the east,

God's beautiful beacon; the billows subsided,

That well I could see the nesses projecting,

Fortune helps the brave earl.

The blustering crags. Weird often saveth

15

The undoomed hero if doughty his valor!

But me did it fortune1 to fell with my weapon

Nine of the nickers. Of night-struggle harder

'Neath dome of the heaven heard I but rarely,

Nor of wight more woful in the waves of the ocean;

20

Yet I 'scaped with my life the grip of the monsters,

After that escape I drifted to Finland.

Weary from travel. Then the waters bare me

To the land of the Finns, the flood with the current,

I have never heard of your doing any such bold deeds.

The weltering waves. Not a word hath been told me

Of deeds so daring done by thee, Unferth,

25

And of sword-terror none; never hath Breca

At the play of the battle, nor either of you two,

Feat so fearless performèd with weapons

Glinting and gleaming . . . .

[22]

. . . . I utter no boasting;

You are a slayer of brothers, and will suffer damnation, wise as you may be.30

Though with cold-blooded cruelty thou killedst thy brothers,

Thy nearest of kin; thou needs must in hell get

Direful damnation, though doughty thy wisdom.

I tell thee in earnest, offspring of Ecglaf,

Never had Grendel such numberless horrors,

35

The direful demon, done to thy liegelord,

Harrying in Heorot, if thy heart were as sturdy,

Had your acts been as brave as your words, Grendel had not ravaged your land so long.

Thy mood as ferocious as thou dost describe them.

He hath found out fully that the fierce-burning hatred,

The edge-battle eager, of all of your kindred,

40

Of the Victory-Scyldings, need little dismay him:

Oaths he exacteth, not any he spares

The monster is not afraid of the Danes,

Of the folk of the Danemen, but fighteth with pleasure,

Killeth and feasteth, no contest expecteth

but he will soon learn to dread the Geats.

From Spear-Danish people. But the prowess and valor

45

Of the earls of the Geatmen early shall venture

To give him a grapple. He shall go who is able

Bravely to banquet, when the bright-light of morning

On the second day, any warrior may go unmolested to the mead-banquet.

Which the second day bringeth, the sun in its ether-robes,

O'er children of men shines from the southward!"

50

Then the gray-haired, war-famed giver of treasure

Hrothgar's spirits are revived.

Was blithesome and joyous, the Bright-Danish ruler

Expected assistance; the people's protector

The old king trusts Beowulf. The heroes are joyful.

Heard from Beowulf his bold resolution.

There was laughter of heroes; loud was the clatter,

55

The words were winsome. Wealhtheow advanced then,

Queen Wealhtheow plays the hostess.

Consort of Hrothgar, of courtesy mindful,

Gold-decked saluted the men in the building,

And the freeborn woman the beaker presented

She offers the cup to her husband first.

To the lord of the kingdom, first of the East-Danes,

60

Bade him be blithesome when beer was a-flowing,

Lief to his liegemen; he lustily tasted

Of banquet and beaker, battle-famed ruler.

The Helmingish lady then graciously circled

'Mid all the liegemen lesser and greater:

[23]She gives presents to the heroes.65

Treasure-cups tendered, till time was afforded

That the decorous-mooded, diademed folk-queen

Then she offers the cup to Beowulf, thanking God that aid has come.

Might bear to Beowulf the bumper o'errunning;

She greeted the Geat-prince, God she did thank,

Most wise in her words, that her wish was accomplished,

70

That in any of earlmen she ever should look for

Solace in sorrow. He accepted the beaker,

Battle-bold warrior, at Wealhtheow's giving,

Beowulf states to the queen the object of his visit.

Then equipped for combat quoth he in measures,

Beowulf spake, offspring of Ecgtheow:

75

"I purposed in spirit when I mounted the ocean,

I determined to do or die.

When I boarded my boat with a band of my liegemen,

I would work to the fullest the will of your people

Or in foe's-clutches fastened fall in the battle.

Deeds I shall do of daring and prowess,

80

Or the last of my life-days live in this mead-hall."

These words to the lady were welcome and pleasing,

The boast of the Geatman; with gold trappings broidered

Went the freeborn folk-queen her fond-lord to sit by.

Glee is high.

Then again as of yore was heard in the building

85

Courtly discussion, conquerors' shouting,

Heroes were happy, till Healfdene's son would

Go to his slumber to seek for refreshing;

For the horrid hell-monster in the hall-building knew he

A fight was determined,2 since the light of the sun they

90

No longer could see, and lowering darkness

O'er all had descended, and dark under heaven

Shadowy shapes came shying around them.

Hrothgar retires, leaving Beowulf in charge of the hall.

The liegemen all rose then. One saluted the other,

Hrothgar Beowulf, in rhythmical measures,

95

Wishing him well, and, the wassail-hall giving

To his care and keeping, quoth he departing:

[24]

"Not to any one else have I ever entrusted,

But thee and thee only, the hall of the Danemen,

Since high I could heave my hand and my buckler.

100

Take thou in charge now the noblest of houses;

Be mindful of honor, exhibiting prowess,

Watch 'gainst the foeman! Thou shalt want no enjoyments,

Survive thou safely adventure so glorious!"

[1] The repetition of 'hwæðere' (574 and 578) is regarded by some scholars as a

defect. B. suggests 'swá Þær' for the first: So there it befell me, etc. Another suggestion is to change the second 'hwæðere' into 'swá Þær': So there I escaped with my life, etc.

[2] Kl. suggests a period after 'determined.' This would give the passage as follows: Since they no longer could see the light of the sun, and lowering darkness was down over all, dire under the heavens shadowy beings came going around them.

XI.

ALL SLEEP SAVE ONE.

Hrothgar retires.

Then Hrothgar departed, his earl-throng attending him,

Folk-lord of Scyldings, forth from the building;

The war-chieftain wished then Wealhtheow to look for,

The queen for a bedmate. To keep away Grendel

God has provided a watch for the hall.5

The Glory of Kings had given a hall-watch,

As men heard recounted: for the king of the Danemen

He did special service, gave the giant a watcher:

And the prince of the Geatmen implicitly trusted

Beowulf is self-confident

His warlike strength and the Wielder's protection.

He prepares for rest.10

His armor of iron off him he did then,

His helmet from his head, to his henchman committed

His chased-handled chain-sword, choicest of weapons,

And bade him bide with his battle-equipments.

The good one then uttered words of defiance,

15

Beowulf Geatman, ere his bed he upmounted:

Beowulf boasts of his ability to cope with Grendel.

"I hold me no meaner in matters of prowess,

In warlike achievements, than Grendel does himself;

Hence I seek not with sword-edge to sooth him to slumber,

Of life to bereave him, though well I am able.

We will fight with nature's weapons only.20

No battle-skill1 has he, that blows he should strike me,

To shatter my shield, though sure he is mighty

[25]

In strife and destruction; but struggling by night we

Shall do without edges, dare he to look for

Weaponless warfare, and wise-mooded Father

25

The glory apportion, God ever-holy,

God may decide who shall conquer

On which hand soever to him seemeth proper."

Then the brave-mooded hero bent to his slumber,

The pillow received the cheek of the noble;

The Geatish warriors lie down.

And many a martial mere-thane attending

30

Sank to his slumber. Seemed it unlikely

They thought it very unlikely that they should ever see their homes again.

That ever thereafter any should hope to

Be happy at home, hero-friends visit

Or the lordly troop-castle where he lived from his childhood;

They had heard how slaughter had snatched from the wine-hall,

35

Had recently ravished, of the race of the Scyldings

But God raised up a deliverer.

Too many by far. But the Lord to them granted

The weaving of war-speed, to Wederish heroes

Aid and comfort, that every opponent

By one man's war-might they worsted and vanquished,

God rules the world.40

By the might of himself; the truth is established

That God Almighty hath governed for ages

Kindreds and nations. A night very lurid

Grendel comes to Heorot.

The trav'ler-at-twilight came tramping and striding.

The warriors were sleeping who should watch the horned-building,

Only one warrior is awake.45

One only excepted. 'Mid earthmen 'twas 'stablished,

Th' implacable foeman was powerless to hurl them

To the land of shadows, if the Lord were unwilling;

But serving as warder, in terror to foemen,

He angrily bided the issue of battle.2

[1] Gr. understood 'gódra' as meaning 'advantages in battle.' This rendering H.-So. rejects. The latter takes the passage as meaning that Grendel, though mighty and formidable, has no skill in the art of war.

[2] B. in his masterly articles on Beowulf (P. and B. XII.) rejects the division

usually made at this point, 'Þá.' (711), usually rendered 'then,' he translates 'when,' and connects its clause with the foregoing sentence. These changes he makes to reduce the number of 'cóm's' as principal verbs. (Cf. 703, 711, 721.) With all deference to this acute scholar, I must say that it seems to me that the poet is exhausting his resources to bring out clearly the supreme event on which the whole subsequent action turns. First, he (Grendel) came in the wan night; second, he came from the moor; third, he came to the hall. Time, place from which, place to which, are all given.

[26]

XII.

GRENDEL AND BEOWULF.

Grendel comes from the fens.

'Neath the cloudy cliffs came from the moor then

Grendel going, God's anger bare he.

The monster intended some one of earthmen

In the hall-building grand to entrap and make way with:

He goes towards the joyous building.5

He went under welkin where well he knew of

The wine-joyous building, brilliant with plating,

Gold-hall of earthmen. Not the earliest occasion

This was not his first visit there.

He the home and manor of Hrothgar had sought:

Ne'er found he in life-days later nor earlier

10

Hardier hero, hall-thanes1 more sturdy!

Then came to the building the warrior marching,

His horrid fingers tear the door open.

Bereft of his joyance. The door quickly opened

On fire-hinges fastened, when his fingers had touched it;

The fell one had flung then—his fury so bitter—

15

Open the entrance. Early thereafter

The foeman trod the shining hall-pavement,

He strides furiously into the hall.

Strode he angrily; from the eyes of him glimmered

A lustre unlovely likest to fire.

He beheld in the hall the heroes in numbers,

20

A circle of kinsmen sleeping together,

He exults over his supposed prey.

A throng of thanemen: then his thoughts were exultant,

He minded to sunder from each of the thanemen

The life from his body, horrible demon,

Ere morning came, since fate had allowed him

Fate has decreed that he shall devour no more heroes. Beowulf suffers from suspense.25

The prospect of plenty. Providence willed not

To permit him any more of men under heaven

To eat in the night-time. Higelac's kinsman

Great sorrow endured how the dire-mooded creature

[27]

In unlooked-for assaults were likely to bear him.

30

No thought had the monster of deferring the matter,

Grendel immediately seizes a sleeping warrior, and devours him.

But on earliest occasion he quickly laid hold of

A soldier asleep, suddenly tore him,

Bit his bone-prison, the blood drank in currents,

Swallowed in mouthfuls: he soon had the dead man's

35

Feet and hands, too, eaten entirely.

Nearer he strode then, the stout-hearted warrior

Beowulf and Grendel grapple.

Snatched as he slumbered, seizing with hand-grip,

Forward the foeman foined with his hand;

Caught he quickly the cunning deviser,

40

On his elbow he rested. This early discovered

The master of malice, that in middle-earth's regions,

'Neath the whole of the heavens, no hand-grapple greater

The monster is amazed at Beowulf's strength.

In any man else had he ever encountered:

Fearful in spirit, faint-mooded waxed he,

45

Not off could betake him; death he was pondering,

He is anxious to flee.

Would fly to his covert, seek the devils' assembly:

His calling no more was the same he had followed

Long in his lifetime. The liege-kinsman worthy

Beowulf recalls his boast of the evening, and determines to fulfil it.

Of Higelac minded his speech of the evening,

50

Stood he up straight and stoutly did seize him.

His fingers crackled; the giant was outward,

The earl stepped farther. The famous one minded

To flee away farther, if he found an occasion,

And off and away, avoiding delay,

55

To fly to the fen-moors; he fully was ware of

The strength of his grapple in the grip of the foeman.

'Twas a luckless day for Grendel.

'Twas an ill-taken journey that the injury-bringing,

Harrying harmer to Heorot wandered:

The hall groans.

The palace re-echoed; to all of the Danemen,

60

Dwellers in castles, to each of the bold ones,

Earlmen, was terror. Angry they both were,

Archwarders raging.2 Rattled the building;

[28]

'Twas a marvellous wonder that the wine-hall withstood then

The bold-in-battle, bent not to earthward,

65

Excellent earth-hall; but within and without it

Was fastened so firmly in fetters of iron,

By the art of the armorer. Off from the sill there

Bent mead-benches many, as men have informed me,

Adorned with gold-work, where the grim ones did struggle.

70

The Scylding wise men weened ne'er before

That by might and main-strength a man under heaven

Might break it in pieces, bone-decked, resplendent,

Crush it by cunning, unless clutch of the fire

In smoke should consume it. The sound mounted upward

Grendel's cries terrify the Danes.75

Novel enough; on the North Danes fastened

A terror of anguish, on all of the men there

Who heard from the wall the weeping and plaining,

The song of defeat from the foeman of heaven,

Heard him hymns of horror howl, and his sorrow

80

Hell-bound bewailing. He held him too firmly

Who was strongest of main-strength of men of that era.

[1] B. and t.B. emend so as to make lines 9 and 10 read: Never in his life, earlier or later, had he, the hell-thane, found a braver hero.—They argue that Beowulf's companions had done nothing to merit such encomiums as the usual readings allow them.

[2] For 'réðe rén-weardas' (771), t.B. suggests 'réðe, rénhearde.' Translate: They were both angry, raging and mighty.

XIII.

GRENDEL IS VANQUISHED.

Beowulf has no idea of letting Grendel live.

For no cause whatever would the earlmen's defender

Leave in life-joys the loathsome newcomer,

He deemed his existence utterly useless

To men under heaven. Many a noble

5

Of Beowulf brandished his battle-sword old,

Would guard the life of his lord and protector,

The far-famed chieftain, if able to do so;

While waging the warfare, this wist they but little,

Brave battle-thanes, while his body intending

No weapon would harm Grendel; he bore a charmed life. 10

To slit into slivers, and seeking his spirit:

That the relentless foeman nor finest of weapons

Of all on the earth, nor any of war-bills

[29]

Was willing to injure; but weapons of victory

Swords and suchlike he had sworn to dispense with.

15

His death at that time must prove to be wretched,

And the far-away spirit widely should journey

Into enemies' power. This plainly he saw then

Who with mirth1 of mood malice no little

Had wrought in the past on the race of the earthmen

20

(To God he was hostile), that his body would fail him,

But Higelac's hardy henchman and kinsman

Held him by the hand; hateful to other

Grendel is sorely wounded.

Was each one if living. A body-wound suffered

The direful demon, damage incurable

His body bursts.25

Was seen on his shoulder, his sinews were shivered,

His body did burst. To Beowulf was given

Glory in battle; Grendel from thenceward

Must flee and hide him in the fen-cliffs and marshes,

Sick unto death, his dwelling must look for

30

Unwinsome and woful; he wist the more fully

The monster flees away to hide in the moors.

The end of his earthly existence was nearing,

His life-days' limits. At last for the Danemen,

When the slaughter was over, their wish was accomplished.

The comer-from-far-land had cleansed then of evil,

35

Wise and valiant, the war-hall of Hrothgar,

Saved it from violence. He joyed in the night-work,

In repute for prowess; the prince of the Geatmen

For the East-Danish people his boast had accomplished,

Bettered their burdensome bale-sorrows fully,

40

The craft-begot evil they erstwhile had suffered

And were forced to endure from crushing oppression,

Their manifold misery. 'Twas a manifest token,

Beowulf suspends Grendel's hand and arm in Heorot.

When the hero-in-battle the hand suspended,

The arm and the shoulder (there was all of the claw

45

Of Grendel together) 'neath great-stretching hall-roof.

[1] It has been proposed to translate 'myrðe' by with sorrow; but there seems no authority for such a rendering. To the present translator, the phrase 'módes myrðe' seems a mere padding for gladly; i.e., he who gladly harassed mankind.

[30]

XIV.

REJOICING OF THE DANES.

At early dawn, warriors from far and near come together to hear of the night's adventures.

In the mist of the morning many a warrior

Stood round the gift-hall, as the story is told me:

Folk-princes fared then from far and from near

Through long-stretching journeys to look at the wonder,

5

The footprints of the foeman. Few of the warriors

Few warriors lamented Grendel's destruction.

Who gazed on the foot-tracks of the inglorious creature

His parting from life pained very deeply,
How, weary in spirit, off from those regions
In combats conquered he carried his traces,
10
Fated and flying, to the flood of the nickers.
Grendel's blood dyes the waters.
There in bloody billows bubbled the currents,
The angry eddy was everywhere mingled
And seething with gore, welling with sword-blood;1
He death-doomed had hid him, when reaved of his joyance
15
He laid down his life in the lair he had fled to,
His heathenish spirit, where hell did receive him.
Thence the friends from of old backward turned them,
And many a younker from merry adventure,
Striding their stallions, stout from the seaward,
20
Heroes on horses. There were heard very often
Beowulf is the hero of the hour.
Beowulf's praises; many often asserted
That neither south nor north, in the circuit of waters,
He is regarded as a probable successor to Hrothgar.
O'er outstretching earth-plain, none other was better
'Mid bearers of war-shields, more worthy to govern,
25
'Neath the arch of the ether. Not any, however,
'Gainst the friend-lord muttered, mocking-words uttered
But no word is uttered to derogate from the old king
Of Hrothgar the gracious (a good king he).
Oft the famed ones permitted their fallow-skinned horses
[31]
To run in rivalry, racing and chasing,
30

68

Where the fieldways appeared to them fair and inviting,
Known for their excellence; oft a thane of the folk-lord,2
The gleeman sings the deeds of heroes.
3A man of celebrity, mindful of rhythms,
Who ancient traditions treasured in memory,
New word-groups found properly bound:
35
The bard after 'gan then Beowulf's venture
He sings in alliterative measures of Beowulf's prowess.
Wisely to tell of, and words that were clever
To utter skilfully, earnestly speaking,
Everything told he that he heard as to Sigmund's
Also of Sigemund, who has slain a great fire-dragon.
Mighty achievements, many things hidden,
40
The strife of the Wælsing, the wide-going ventures
The children of men knew of but little,
The feud and the fury, but Fitela with him,
When suchlike matters he minded to speak of,
Uncle to nephew, as in every contention
45
Each to other was ever devoted:
A numerous host of the race of the scathers
They had slain with the sword-edge. To Sigmund accrued then
No little of glory, when his life-days were over,
Since he sturdy in struggle had destroyed the great dragon,
50
The hoard-treasure's keeper; 'neath the hoar-grayish stone he,
The son of the atheling, unaided adventured
The perilous project; not present was Fitela,
Yet the fortune befell him of forcing his weapon
Through the marvellous dragon, that it stood in the wall,
55
Well-honored weapon; the worm was slaughtered.
The great one had gained then by his glorious achievement
To reap from the ring-hoard richest enjoyment,
[32]
As best it did please him: his vessel he loaded,
Shining ornaments on the ship's bosom carried,
60

Kinsman of Wæls: the drake in heat melted.
Sigemund was widely famed.
He was farthest famed of fugitive pilgrims,
Mid wide-scattered world-folk, for works of great prowess,
War-troopers' shelter: hence waxed he in honor.4
Heremod, an unfortunate Danish king, is introduced by way of contrast.
Afterward Heremod's hero-strength failed him,
65
His vigor and valor. 'Mid venomous haters
To the hands of foemen he was foully delivered,
Offdriven early. Agony-billows
Unlike Sigemund and Beowulf, Heremod was a burden to his people.
Oppressed him too long, to his people he became then,
To all the athelings, an ever-great burden;
70
And the daring one's journey in days of yore
Many wise men were wont to deplore,
Such as hoped he would bring them help in their sorrow,
That the son of their ruler should rise into power,
Holding the headship held by his fathers,
75
Should govern the people, the gold-hoard and borough,
The kingdom of heroes, the realm of the Scyldings.

Beowulf is an honor to his race.
He to all men became then far more beloved,
Higelac's kinsman, to kindreds and races,
To his friends much dearer; him malice assaulted.—
The story is resumed.80
Oft running and racing on roadsters they measured
The dun-colored highways. Then the light of the morning
Was hurried and hastened. Went henchmen in numbers
To the beautiful building, bold ones in spirit,
To look at the wonder; the liegelord himself then
85
From his wife-bower wending, warden of treasures,
Glorious trod with troopers unnumbered,
Famed for his virtues, and with him the queen-wife
Measured the mead-ways, with maidens attending.
[1] S. emends, suggesting 'déop' for 'déog,' and removing semicolon after 'wéol.'
The two half-lines 'welling … hid him' would then read: The bloody deep welled
with sword-gore. B. accepts 'déop' for 'déog,' but reads 'déað-fæges': The deep
boiled with the sword-gore of the death-doomed one.
[2] Another and quite different rendering of this passage is as follows: Oft a
liegeman of the king, a fame-covered man mindful of songs, who very many
ancient traditions remembered (he found other word-groups accurately bound
together) began afterward to tell of Beowulf's adventure, skilfully to narrate it,
etc.
[3] Might 'guma gilp-hladen' mean 'a man laden with boasts of the deeds of
others'?
[4] t.B. accepts B.'s 'hé þæs áron þáh' as given by H.-So., but puts a comma after
'þáh,' and takes 'siððan' as introducing a dependent clause: He throve in honor
since Heremod's strength … had decreased.
[33]
XV.
HROTHGAR'S GRATITUDE.

Hrothgar discoursed (to the hall-building went he,
He stood by the pillar,1 saw the steep-rising hall-roof
Gleaming with gold-gems, and Grendel his hand there):
Hrothgar gives thanks for the overthrow of the monster.
"For the sight we behold now, thanks to the Wielder
5
Early be offered! Much evil I bided,
Snaring from Grendel:2 God can e'er 'complish
Wonder on wonder, Wielder of Glory!
I had given up all hope, when this brave liegeman came to our aid.
But lately I reckoned ne'er under heaven
Comfort to gain me for any of sorrows,

71

10
While the handsomest of houses horrid with bloodstain
Gory uptowered; grief had offfrightened3
Each of the wise ones who weened not that ever
The folk-troop's defences 'gainst foes they should strengthen,
'Gainst sprites and monsters. Through the might of the Wielder
15
A doughty retainer hath a deed now accomplished
Which erstwhile we all with our excellent wisdom
If his mother yet liveth, well may she thank God for this son.
Failed to perform. May affirm very truly
What woman soever in all of the nations
Gave birth to the child, if yet she surviveth,
20
That the long-ruling Lord was lavish to herward
In the birth of the bairn. Now, Beowulf dear,
Hereafter, Beowulf, thou shalt be my son.
Most excellent hero, I'll love thee in spirit
As bairn of my body; bear well henceforward
The relationship new. No lack shall befall thee
25
Of earth-joys any I ever can give thee.
Full often for lesser service I've given
[34]
Hero less hardy hoard-treasure precious,
Thou hast won immortal distinction.
To a weaker in war-strife. By works of distinction
Thou hast gained for thyself now that thy glory shall flourish
30
Forever and ever. The All-Ruler quite thee
With good from His hand as He hitherto did thee!"
Beowulf replies: I was most happy to render thee this service.
Beowulf answered, Ecgtheow's offspring:
"That labor of glory most gladly achieved we,
The combat accomplished, unquailing we ventured
35
The enemy's grapple; I would grant it much rather
Thou wert able to look at the creature in person,
Faint unto falling, the foe in his trappings!
On murder-bed quickly I minded to bind him,
With firm-holding fetters, that forced by my grapple
40
Low he should lie in life-and-death struggle
'Less his body escape; I was wholly unable,
I could not keep the monster from escaping, as God did not will that I should.

Since God did not will it, to keep him from going,
Not held him that firmly, hated opposer;
Too swift was the foeman. Yet safety regarding
45
He suffered his hand behind him to linger,
His arm and shoulder, to act as watcher;
He left his hand and arm behind.
No shadow of solace the woe-begone creature
Found him there nathless: the hated destroyer
Liveth no longer, lashed for his evils,
50
But sorrow hath seized him, in snare-meshes hath him
Close in its clutches, keepeth him writhing
In baleful bonds: there banished for evil
The man shall wait for the mighty tribunal,
God will give him his deserts.
How the God of glory shall give him his earnings."
55
Then the soldier kept silent, son of old Ecglaf,
Unferth has nothing more to say, for Beowulf's actions speak louder than words.
From boasting and bragging of battle-achievements,
Since the princes beheld there the hand that depended
'Neath the lofty hall-timbers by the might of the nobleman,
Each one before him, the enemy's fingers;
60
Each finger-nail strong steel most resembled,
The heathen one's hand-spur, the hero-in-battle's
Claw most uncanny; quoth they agreeing,
[35]No sword will harm the monster.
That not any excellent edges of brave ones
Was willing to touch him, the terrible creature's
65
Battle-hand bloody to bear away from him.
[1] B. and t.B. read 'staþole,' and translate stood on the floor.
[2] For 'snaring from Grendel,' 'sorrows at Grendel's hands' has been suggested.
This gives a parallel to 'láðes.' 'Grynna' may well be gen. pl. of 'gyrn,' by a
scribal slip.
[3] The H.-So punctuation has been followed; but B. has been followed in
understanding 'gehwylcne' as object of 'wíd-scofen (hæfde).' Gr. construes 'wéa'
as nom abs.
XVI.
HROTHGAR LAVISHES GIFTS UPON HIS DELIVERER.

Heorot is adorned with hands.
Then straight was ordered that Heorot inside1

With hands be embellished: a host of them gathered,
Of men and women, who the wassailing-building
The guest-hall begeared. Gold-flashing sparkled
5
Webs on the walls then, of wonders a many
To each of the heroes that look on such objects.
The hall is defaced, however.
The beautiful building was broken to pieces
Which all within with irons was fastened,
Its hinges torn off: only the roof was
10
Whole and uninjured when the horrible creature
Outlawed for evil off had betaken him,
Hopeless of living. 'Tis hard to avoid it
[A vague passage of five verses.]
(Whoever will do it!); but he doubtless must come to2
The place awaiting, as Wyrd hath appointed,
15
Soul-bearers, earth-dwellers, earls under heaven,
Where bound on its bed his body shall slumber
Hrothgar goes to the banquet.
When feasting is finished. Full was the time then
That the son of Healfdene went to the building;
[36]
The excellent atheling would eat of the banquet.
20
Ne'er heard I that people with hero-band larger
Bare them better tow'rds their bracelet-bestower.
The laden-with-glory stooped to the bench then
(Their kinsmen-companions in plenty were joyful,
Many a cupful quaffing complaisantly),
25
Doughty of spirit in the high-tow'ring palace,
Hrothgar's nephew, Hrothulf, is present.
Hrothgar and Hrothulf. Heorot then inside
Was filled with friendly ones; falsehood and treachery
The Folk-Scyldings now nowise did practise.
Hrothgar lavishes gifts upon Beowulf.
Then the offspring of Healfdene offered to Beowulf
30
A golden standard, as reward for the victory,
A banner embossed, burnie and helmet;
Many men saw then a song-famous weapon
Borne 'fore the hero. Beowulf drank of
The cup in the building; that treasure-bestowing

35
He needed not blush for in battle-men's presence.
Four handsomer gifts were never presented.
Ne'er heard I that many men on the ale-bench
In friendlier fashion to their fellows presented
Four bright jewels with gold-work embellished.
'Round the roof of the helmet a head-guarder outside
40
Braided with wires, with bosses was furnished,
That swords-for-the-battle fight-hardened might fail
Boldly to harm him, when the hero proceeded
Hrothgar commands that eight finely caparisoned steeds be brought to Beowulf.
Forth against foemen. The defender of earls then
Commanded that eight steeds with bridles
45
Gold-plated, gleaming, be guided to hallward,
Inside the building; on one of them stood then
An art-broidered saddle embellished with jewels;
'Twas the sovereign's seat, when the son of King Healfdene
Was pleased to take part in the play of the edges;
50
The famous one's valor ne'er failed at the front when
Slain ones were bowing. And to Beowulf granted
The prince of the Ingwins, power over both,
O'er war-steeds and weapons; bade him well to enjoy them.
In so manly a manner the mighty-famed chieftain,
[37]55
Hoard-ward of heroes, with horses and jewels
War-storms requited, that none e'er condemneth
Who willeth to tell truth with full justice.
[1] Kl. suggests 'hroden' for 'háten,' and renders: Then quickly was Heorot adorned within, with hands bedecked.—B. suggests 'gefrætwon' instead of 'gefrætwod,' and renders: Then was it commanded to adorn Heorot within quickly with hands.—The former has the advantage of affording a parallel to 'gefrætwod': both have the disadvantage of altering the text.
[2] The passage 1005-1009 seems to be hopeless. One difficult point is to find a subject for 'gesacan.' Some say 'he'; others supply 'each,' i.e., every soul-bearer … must gain the inevitable place. The genitives in this case are partitive.—If 'he' be subj., the genitives are dependent on 'gearwe' (= prepared).—The 'he' itself is disputed, some referring it to Grendel; but B. takes it as involved in the parenthesis.
XVII.
BANQUET (continued).—THE SCOP'S SONG OF FINN AND HNÆF.

Each of Beowulf's companions receives a costly gift.

And the atheling of earlmen to each of the heroes
Who the ways of the waters went with Beowulf,
A costly gift-token gave on the mead-bench,
Offered an heirloom, and ordered that that man
The warrior killed by Grendel is to be paid for in gold.5
With gold should be paid for, whom Grendel had erstwhile
Wickedly slaughtered, as he more of them had done
Had far-seeing God and the mood of the hero
The fate not averted: the Father then governed
All of the earth-dwellers, as He ever is doing;
10
Hence insight for all men is everywhere fittest,
Forethought of spirit! much he shall suffer
Of lief and of loathsome who long in this present
Useth the world in this woful existence.
There was music and merriment mingling together
Hrothgar's scop recalls events in the reign of his lord's father.15
Touching Healfdene's leader; the joy-wood was fingered,
Measures recited, when the singer of Hrothgar
On mead-bench should mention the merry hall-joyance
Of the kinsmen of Finn, when onset surprised them:
Hnæf, the Danish general, is treacherously attacked while staying at Finn's castle.
"The Half-Danish hero, Hnæf of the Scyldings,
20
On the field of the Frisians was fated to perish.
Sure Hildeburg needed not mention approving
The faith of the Jutemen: though blameless entirely,
Queen Hildeburg is not only wife of Finn, but a kinswoman of the murdered Hnæf.
When shields were shivered she was shorn of her darlings,
Of bairns and brothers: they bent to their fate
25
With war-spear wounded; woe was that woman.
Not causeless lamented the daughter of Hoce
The decree of the Wielder when morning-light came and
She was able 'neath heaven to behold the destruction
[38]
Of brothers and bairns, where the brightest of earth-joys
Finn's force is almost exterminated.30
She had hitherto had: all the henchmen of Finn
War had offtaken, save a handful remaining,
That he nowise was able to offer resistance1
Hengest succeeds Hnæf as Danish general.
To the onset of Hengest in the parley of battle,
Nor the wretched remnant to rescue in war from

76

35
The earl of the atheling; but they offered conditions,
Compact between the Frisians and the Danes.
Another great building to fully make ready,
A hall and a high-seat, that half they might rule with
The sons of the Jutemen, and that Folcwalda's son would
Day after day the Danemen honor
40
When gifts were giving, and grant of his ring-store
To Hengest's earl-troop ever so freely,
Of his gold-plated jewels, as he encouraged the Frisians
Equality of gifts agreed on.
On the bench of the beer-hall. On both sides they swore then
A fast-binding compact; Finn unto Hengest
45
With no thought of revoking vowed then most solemnly
The woe-begone remnant well to take charge of,
His Witan advising; the agreement should no one
By words or works weaken and shatter,
By artifice ever injure its value,
50
Though reaved of their ruler their ring-giver's slayer
They followed as vassals, Fate so requiring:
No one shall refer to old grudges.
Then if one of the Frisians the quarrel should speak of
In tones that were taunting, terrible edges
Should cut in requital. Accomplished the oath was,
55
And treasure of gold from the hoard was uplifted.
Danish warriors are burned on a funeral-pyre.
The best of the Scylding braves was then fully
Prepared for the pile; at the pyre was seen clearly
The blood-gory burnie, the boar with his gilding,
The iron-hard swine, athelings many
60
Fatally wounded; no few had been slaughtered.
Hildeburg bade then, at the burning of Hnæf,
[39]Queen Hildeburg has her son burnt along with Hnæf.
The bairn of her bosom to bear to the fire,
That his body be burned and borne to the pyre.
The woe-stricken woman wept on his shoulder,2
65
In measures lamented; upmounted the hero.3
The greatest of dead-fires curled to the welkin,
On the hill's-front crackled; heads were a-melting,

Wound-doors bursting, while the blood was a-coursing
From body-bite fierce. The fire devoured them,
70
Greediest of spirits, whom war had offcarried
From both of the peoples; their bravest were fallen.

[1] For 1084, R. suggests 'wiht Hengeste wið gefeohtan.'—K. suggests 'wið Hengeste wiht gefeohtan.' Neither emendation would make any essential change in the translation.

[2] The separation of adjective and noun by a phrase (cf. v. 1118) being very unusual, some scholars have put 'earme on eaxle' with the foregoing lines, inserting a semicolon after 'eaxle.' In this case 'on eaxe' (i.e., on the ashes, cinders) is sometimes read, and this affords a parallel to 'on bæl.' Let us hope that a satisfactory rendering shall yet be reached without resorting to any tampering with the text, such as Lichtenheld proposed: 'earme ides on eaxle gnornode.'

[3] For 'gúð-rinc,' 'gúð-réc,' battle-smoke, has been suggested.

XVIII.

THE FINN EPISODE (continued).—THE BANQUET CONTINUES.

The survivors go to Friesland, the home of Finn.
"Then the warriors departed to go to their dwellings,
Reaved of their friends, Friesland to visit,
Their homes and high-city. Hengest continued
Hengest remains there all winter, unable to get away.
Biding with Finn the blood-tainted winter,
5
Wholly unsundered;1 of fatherland thought he
Though unable to drive the ring-stemmèd vessel
[40]
O'er the ways of the waters; the wave-deeps were tossing,
Fought with the wind; winter in ice-bonds
Closed up the currents, till there came to the dwelling
10
A year in its course, as yet it revolveth,
If season propitious one alway regardeth,
World-cheering weathers. Then winter was gone,
Earth's bosom was lovely; the exile would get him,
He devises schemes of vengeance.
The guest from the palace; on grewsomest vengeance
15
He brooded more eager than on oversea journeys,
Whe'r onset-of-anger he were able to 'complish,
The bairns of the Jutemen therein to remember.
Nowise refused he the duties of liegeman
When Hun of the Frisians the battle-sword Láfing,
20

Fairest of falchions, friendly did give him:
Its edges were famous in folk-talk of Jutland.
And savage sword-fury seized in its clutches
Bold-mooded Finn where he bode in his palace,
Guthlaf and Oslaf revenge Hnæf's slaughter.
When the grewsome grapple Guthlaf and Oslaf
25
Had mournfully mentioned, the mere-journey over,
For sorrows half-blamed him; the flickering spirit
Could not bide in his bosom. Then the building was covered2
Finn is slain.

With corpses of foemen, and Finn too was slaughtered,
The king with his comrades, and the queen made a prisoner.
The jewels of Finn, and his queen are carried away by the Danes.30
The troops of the Scyldings bore to their vessels
All that the land-king had in his palace,
Such trinkets and treasures they took as, on searching,
At Finn's they could find. They ferried to Daneland
The excellent woman on oversea journey,
The lay is concluded, and the main story is resumed.35
Led her to their land-folk." The lay was concluded,
The gleeman's recital. Shouts again rose then,
Bench-glee resounded, bearers then offered
Skinkers carry round the beaker.
Wine from wonder-vats. Wealhtheo advanced then
Going 'neath gold-crown, where the good ones were seated
[41]Queen Wealhtheow greets Hrothgar, as he sits beside Hrothulf, his nephew.40
Uncle and nephew; their peace was yet mutual,

True each to the other. And Unferth the spokesman
Sat at the feet of the lord of the Scyldings:
Each trusted his spirit that his mood was courageous,
Though at fight he had failed in faith to his kinsmen.
45
Said the queen of the Scyldings: "My lord and protector,
Treasure-bestower, take thou this beaker;
Joyance attend thee, gold-friend of heroes,
Be generous to the Geats.
And greet thou the Geatmen with gracious responses!
So ought one to do. Be kind to the Geatmen,
50
In gifts not niggardly; anear and afar now
Peace thou enjoyest. Report hath informed me
Thou'lt have for a bairn the battle-brave hero.
Now is Heorot cleansèd, ring-palace gleaming;
Have as much joy as possible in thy hall, once more purified.
Give while thou mayest many rewards,
55
And bequeath to thy kinsmen kingdom and people,
On wending thy way to the Wielder's splendor.
I know good Hrothulf, that the noble young troopers
I know that Hrothulf will prove faithful if he survive thee.
He'll care for and honor, lord of the Scyldings,
If earth-joys thou endest earlier than he doth;
60
I reckon that recompense he'll render with kindness
Our offspring and issue, if that all he remember,
What favors of yore, when he yet was an infant,
We awarded to him for his worship and pleasure."
Then she turned by the bench where her sons were carousing,
65
Hrethric and Hrothmund, and the heroes' offspring,
Beowulf is sitting by the two royal sons.
The war-youth together; there the good one was sitting
'Twixt the brothers twain, Beowulf Geatman.
[1] For 1130 (1) R. and Gr. suggest 'elne unflitme' as 1098 (1) reads. The latter verse is undisputed; and, for the former, 'elne' would be as possible as 'ealles,' and 'unflitme' is well supported. Accepting 'elne unflitme' for both, I would suggest 'very peaceably' for both places: (1) Finn to Hengest very peaceably vowed with oaths, etc. (2) Hengest then still the slaughter-stained winter remained there with Finn very peaceably. The two passages become thus correlatives, the second a sequel of the first. 'Elne,' in the sense of very (swíðe), needs no argument; and 'unflitme' (from 'flítan') can, it seems to me, be more plausibly rendered 'peaceful,' 'peaceable,' than 'contestable,' or 'conquerable.'

[2] Some scholars have proposed 'roden'; the line would then read: Then the building was reddened, etc., instead of 'covered.' The 'h' may have been carried over from the three alliterating 'h's.'

XIX.

BEOWULF RECEIVES FURTHER HONOR.

More gifts are offered Beowulf.

A beaker was borne him, and bidding to quaff it
Graciously given, and gold that was twisted
Pleasantly proffered, a pair of arm-jewels,
[42]
Rings and corslet, of collars the greatest
5
I've heard of 'neath heaven. Of heroes not any
More splendid from jewels have I heard 'neath the welkin,

A famous necklace is referred to, in comparison with the gems presented to Beowulf.

Since Hama off bore the Brosingmen's necklace,
The bracteates and jewels, from the bright-shining city,1
Eormenric's cunning craftiness fled from,
10
Chose gain everlasting. Geatish Higelac,
Grandson of Swerting, last had this jewel
When tramping 'neath banner the treasure he guarded,
The field-spoil defended; Fate offcarried him
When for deeds of daring he endured tribulation,
15
Hate from the Frisians; the ornaments bare he
O'er the cup of the currents, costly gem-treasures,
Mighty folk-leader, he fell 'neath his target;
The2 corpse of the king then came into charge of
The race of the Frankmen, the mail-shirt and collar:
20
Warmen less noble plundered the fallen,
When the fight was finished; the folk of the Geatmen
The field of the dead held in possession.
The choicest of mead-halls with cheering resounded.
Wealhtheo discoursed, the war-troop addressed she:

Queen Wealhtheow magnifies Beowulf's achievements.25

"This collar enjoy thou, Beowulf worthy,
Young man, in safety, and use thou this armor,
Gems of the people, and prosper thou fully,
Show thyself sturdy and be to these liegemen
Mild with instruction! I'll mind thy requital.
30

Thou hast brought it to pass that far and near
Forever and ever earthmen shall honor thee,
Even so widely as ocean surroundeth
The blustering bluffs. Be, while thou livest,
[43]
A wealth-blessèd atheling. I wish thee most truly
May gifts never fail thee.35
Jewels and treasure. Be kind to my son, thou
Living in joyance! Here each of the nobles
Is true unto other, gentle in spirit,
Loyal to leader. The liegemen are peaceful,
The war-troops ready: well-drunken heroes,3
40
Do as I bid ye." Then she went to the settle.
There was choicest of banquets, wine drank the heroes:
They little know of the sorrow in store for them.
Weird they knew not, destiny cruel,
As to many an earlman early it happened,
When evening had come and Hrothgar had parted
45
Off to his manor, the mighty to slumber.
Warriors unnumbered warded the building
As erst they did often: the ale-settle bared they,
'Twas covered all over with beds and pillows.
A doomed thane is there with them.
Doomed unto death, down to his slumber
50
Bowed then a beer-thane. Their battle-shields placed they,
Bright-shining targets, up by their heads then;
O'er the atheling on ale-bench 'twas easy to see there
Battle-high helmet, burnie of ring-mail,
They were always ready for battle.
And mighty war-spear. 'Twas the wont of that people
55
To constantly keep them equipped for the battle,4
At home or marching—in either condition—
At seasons just such as necessity ordered
As best for their ruler; that people was worthy.

[1] C. suggests a semicolon after 'city,' with 'he' as supplied subject of 'fled' and 'chose.'
[2] For 'feorh' S. suggests 'feoh': 'corpse' in the translation would then be changed to 'possessions,' 'belongings.' This is a better reading than one joining, in such intimate syntactical relations, things so unlike as 'corpse' and 'jewels.'
[3] S. suggests 'wine-joyous heroes,' 'warriors elated with wine.'
[4] I believe this translation brings out the meaning of the poet, without departing

seriously from the H.-So. text. 'Oft' frequently means 'constantly,' 'continually,' not always 'often.'—Why 'an (on) wíg gearwe' should be written 'ánwíg-gearwe' (= ready for single combat), I cannot see. 'Gearwe' occurs quite frequently with 'on'; cf. B. 1110 (ready for the pyre), El. 222 (ready for the glad journey). Moreover, what has the idea of single combat to do with B. 1247 ff.? The poet is giving an inventory of the arms and armor which they lay aside on retiring, and he closes his narration by saying that they were always prepared for battle both at home and on the march.

[44]

XX.

THE MOTHER OF GRENDEL.

They sank then to slumber. With sorrow one paid for
His evening repose, as often betid them
While Grendel was holding1 the gold-bedecked palace,
Ill-deeds performing, till his end overtook him,
5
Death for his sins. 'Twas seen very clearly,
Grendel's mother is known to be thirsting for revenge.
Known unto earth-folk, that still an avenger
Outlived the loathed one, long since the sorrow
Caused by the struggle; the mother of Grendel,
Devil-shaped woman, her woe ever minded,
10
Who was held to inhabit the horrible waters,
[Grendel's progenitor, Cain, is again referred to.]
The cold-flowing currents, after Cain had become a
Slayer-with-edges to his one only brother,
The son of his sire; he set out then banished,
Marked as a murderer, man-joys avoiding,
15
Lived in the desert. Thence demons unnumbered
The poet again magnifies Beowulf's valor.
Fate-sent awoke; one of them Grendel,
Sword-cursèd, hateful, who at Heorot met with
A man that was watching, waiting the struggle,
Where a horrid one held him with hand-grapple sturdy;
20
Nathless he minded the might of his body,
The glorious gift God had allowed him,
And folk-ruling Father's favor relied on,
His help and His comfort: so he conquered the foeman,
The hell-spirit humbled: he unhappy departed then,
25
Reaved of his joyance, journeying to death-haunts,

Foeman of man. His mother moreover
Grendel's mother comes to avenge her son.
Eager and gloomy was anxious to go on
Her mournful mission, mindful of vengeance
For the death of her son. She came then to Heorot
[45]30
Where the Armor-Dane earlmen all through the building
Were lying in slumber. Soon there became then
Return2 to the nobles, when the mother of Grendel
Entered the folk-hall; the fear was less grievous
By even so much as the vigor of maidens,
35
War-strength of women, by warrior is reckoned,
When well-carved weapon, worked with the hammer,
Blade very bloody, brave with its edges,
Strikes down the boar-sign that stands on the helmet.
Then the hard-edgèd weapon was heaved in the building,3
40
The brand o'er the benches, broad-lindens many
Hand-fast were lifted; for helmet he recked not,
For armor-net broad, whom terror laid hold of.
She went then hastily, outward would get her
Her life for to save, when some one did spy her;
She seizes a favorite liegemen of Hrothgar's.45
Soon she had grappled one of the athelings
Fast and firmly, when fenward she hied her;
That one to Hrothgar was liefest of heroes
In rank of retainer where waters encircle,
A mighty shield-warrior, whom she murdered at slumber,
50
A broadly-famed battle-knight. Beowulf was absent,
Beowulf was asleep in another part of the palace.
But another apartment was erstwhile devoted
To the glory-decked Geatman when gold was distributed.
There was hubbub in Heorot. The hand that was famous
She grasped in its gore;4 grief was renewed then
[46]55
In homes and houses: 'twas no happy arrangement
In both of the quarters to barter and purchase
With lives of their friends. Then the well-agèd ruler,
The gray-headed war-thane, was woful in spirit,
When his long-trusted liegeman lifeless he knew of,
Beowulf is sent for.60
His dearest one gone. Quick from a room was
Beowulf brought, brave and triumphant.

As day was dawning in the dusk of the morning,
He comes at Hrothgar's summons.
Went then that earlman, champion noble,
Came with comrades, where the clever one bided
65
Whether God all gracious would grant him a respite
After the woe he had suffered. The war-worthy hero
With a troop of retainers trod then the pavement
(The hall-building groaned), till he greeted the wise one,
Beowulf inquires how Hrothgar had enjoyed his night's rest.
The earl of the Ingwins;5 asked if the night had
70
Fully refreshed him, as fain he would have it.

[1] Several eminent authorities either read or emend the MS. so as to make this verse read, While Grendel was wasting the gold-bedecked palace. So 20 15 below: ravaged the desert.

[2] For 'sóna' (1281), t.B. suggests 'sára,' limiting 'edhwyrft.' Read then: Return of sorrows to the nobles, etc. This emendation supplies the syntactical gap after 'edhwyrft.'

[3] Some authorities follow Grein's lexicon in treating 'heard ecg' as an adj. limiting 'sweord': H.-So. renders it as a subst. (So v. 1491.) The sense of the translation would be the same.

[4] B. suggests 'under hróf genam' (v. 1303). This emendation, as well as an emendation with (?) to v. 739, he offers, because 'under' baffles him in both passages. All we need is to take 'under' in its secondary meaning of 'in,' which, though not given by Grein, occurs in the literature. Cf. Chron. 876 (March's A.-S. Gram. § 355) and Oro. Amaz. I. 10, where 'under' = in the midst of. Cf. modern Eng. 'in such circumstances,' which interchanges in good usage with 'under such circumstances.'

[5] For 'néod-laðu' (1321) C. suggests 'néad-láðum,' and translates: asked whether the night had been pleasant to him after crushing-hostility.

XXI.
HROTHGAR'S ACCOUNT OF THE MONSTERS.

Hrothgar laments the death of Æschere, his shoulder-companion.
Hrothgar rejoined, helm of the Scyldings:
"Ask not of joyance! Grief is renewed to
The folk of the Danemen. Dead is Æschere,
Yrmenlaf's brother, older than he,
5
My true-hearted counsellor, trusty adviser,
Shoulder-companion, when fighting in battle
Our heads we protected, when troopers were clashing,
He was my ideal hero.
And heroes were dashing; such an earl should be ever,

An erst-worthy atheling, as Æschere proved him.
10
The flickering death-spirit became in Heorot
His hand-to-hand murderer; I can not tell whither
The cruel one turned in the carcass exulting,
[47]This horrible creature came to avenge Grendel's death.
By cramming discovered.1 The quarrel she wreaked then,

That last night igone Grendel thou killedst
15
In grewsomest manner, with grim-holding clutches,
Since too long he had lessened my liege-troop and wasted
My folk-men so foully. He fell in the battle
With forfeit of life, and another has followed,
A mighty crime-worker, her kinsman avenging,
20
And henceforth hath 'stablished her hatred unyielding,2
As it well may appear to many a liegeman,
Who mourneth in spirit the treasure-bestower,
Her heavy heart-sorrow; the hand is now lifeless
Which3 availed you in every wish that you cherished.
I have heard my vassals speak of these two uncanny monsters who lived in the moors.25
Land-people heard I, liegemen, this saying,
Dwellers in halls, they had seen very often
A pair of such mighty march-striding creatures,
Far-dwelling spirits, holding the moorlands:

86

One of them wore, as well they might notice,
30
The image of woman, the other one wretched
In guise of a man wandered in exile,
Except he was huger than any of earthmen;
Earth-dwelling people entitled him Grendel
In days of yore: they know not their father,
35
Whe'r ill-going spirits any were borne him
The inhabit the most desolate and horrible places.
Ever before. They guard the wolf-coverts,
Lands inaccessible, wind-beaten nesses,
Fearfullest fen-deeps, where a flood from the mountains
'Neath mists of the nesses netherward rattles,
40
The stream under earth: not far is it henceward
Measured by mile-lengths that the mere-water standeth,
Which forests hang over, with frost-whiting covered,4
[48]
A firm-rooted forest, the floods overshadow.
There ever at night one an ill-meaning portent
45
A fire-flood may see; 'mong children of men
None liveth so wise that wot of the bottom;
Though harassed by hounds the heath-stepper seek for,
Even the hounded deer will not seek refuge in these uncanny regions.
Fly to the forest, firm-antlered he-deer,
Spurred from afar, his spirit he yieldeth,
50
His life on the shore, ere in he will venture
To cover his head. Uncanny the place is:
Thence upward ascendeth the surging of waters,
Wan to the welkin, when the wind is stirring
The weathers unpleasing, till the air groweth gloomy,
To thee only can I look for assistance.55
And the heavens lower. Now is help to be gotten
From thee and thee only! The abode thou know'st not,
The dangerous place where thou'rt able to meet with
The sin-laden hero: seek if thou darest!
For the feud I will fully fee thee with money,
60
With old-time treasure, as erstwhile I did thee,
With well-twisted jewels, if away thou shalt get thee."
[1] For 'gefrægnod' (1334), K. and t.B. suggest 'gefægnod,' rendering 'rejoicing
in her fill.' This gives a parallel to 'æse wlanc' (1333).

[2] The line 'And … yielding,' B. renders: And she has performed a deed of blood-vengeance whose effect is far-reaching.

[3] 'Sé Þe' (1345) is an instance of masc. rel. with fem. antecedent. So v. 1888, where 'sé Þe' refers to 'yldo.'

[4] For 'hrímge' in the H.-So. edition, Gr. and others read 'hrínde' (=hrínende), and translate: which rustling forests overhang.

XXII.

BEOWULF SEEKS GRENDEL'S MOTHER.

Beowulf answered, Ecgtheow's son:

Beowulf exhorts the old king to arouse himself for action.

"Grieve not, O wise one! for each it is better,
His friend to avenge than with vehemence wail him;
Each of us must the end-day abide of
5
His earthly existence; who is able accomplish
Glory ere death! To battle-thane noble
Lifeless lying, 'tis at last most fitting.
Arise, O king, quick let us hasten
To look at the footprint of the kinsman of Grendel!
10
I promise thee this now: to his place he'll escape not,
To embrace of the earth, nor to mountainous forest,
Nor to depths of the ocean, wherever he wanders.
[49]
Practice thou now patient endurance
Of each of thy sorrows, as I hope for thee soothly!"
Hrothgar rouses himself. His horse is brought.15
Then up sprang the old one, the All-Wielder thanked he,
Ruler Almighty, that the man had outspoken.
Then for Hrothgar a war-horse was decked with a bridle,
Curly-maned courser. The clever folk-leader

They start on the track of the female monster.

Stately proceeded: stepped then an earl-troop
20
Of linden-wood bearers. Her footprints were seen then
Widely in wood-paths, her way o'er the bottoms,
Where she faraway fared o'er fen-country murky,
Bore away breathless the best of retainers
Who pondered with Hrothgar the welfare of country.
25
The son of the athelings then went o'er the stony,
Declivitous cliffs, the close-covered passes,
Narrow passages, paths unfrequented,
Nesses abrupt, nicker-haunts many;

One of a few of wise-mooded heroes,
30
He onward advanced to view the surroundings,
Till he found unawares woods of the mountain
O'er hoar-stones hanging, holt-wood unjoyful;
The water stood under, welling and gory.
'Twas irksome in spirit to all of the Danemen,
35
Friends of the Scyldings, to many a liegeman
The sight of Æschere's head causes them great sorrow.
Sad to be suffered, a sorrow unlittle
To each of the earlmen, when to Æschere's head they
Came on the cliff. The current was seething
With blood and with gore (the troopers gazed on it).
40
The horn anon sang the battle-song ready.
The troop were all seated; they saw 'long the water then
The water is filled with serpents and sea-dragons.
Many a serpent, mere-dragons wondrous
Trying the waters, nickers a-lying
On the cliffs of the nesses, which at noonday full often
45
Go on the sea-deeps their sorrowful journey,
Wild-beasts and wormkind; away then they hastened
One of them is killed by Beowulf.
Hot-mooded, hateful, they heard the great clamor,
The war-trumpet winding. One did the Geat-prince
[50]
Sunder from earth-joys, with arrow from bowstring,
50
From his sea-struggle tore him, that the trusty war-missile
The dead beast is a poor swimmer
Pierced to his vitals; he proved in the currents
Less doughty at swimming whom death had offcarried.
Soon in the waters the wonderful swimmer
Was straitened most sorely with sword-pointed boar-spears,
55

Pressed in the battle and pulled to the cliff-edge;
The liegemen then looked on the loath-fashioned stranger.
Beowulf prepares for a struggle with the monster.
Beowulf donned then his battle-equipments,
Cared little for life; inlaid and most ample,
The hand-woven corslet which could cover his body,
60
Must the wave-deeps explore, that war might be powerless
To harm the great hero, and the hating one's grasp might
Not peril his safety; his head was protected
By the light-flashing helmet that should mix with the bottoms,
Trying the eddies, treasure-emblazoned,
65
Encircled with jewels, as in seasons long past
The weapon-smith worked it, wondrously made it,
With swine-bodies fashioned it, that thenceforward no longer
Brand might bite it, and battle-sword hurt it.
And that was not least of helpers in prowess
He has Unferth's sword in his hand.70
That Hrothgar's spokesman had lent him when straitened;
And the hilted hand-sword was Hrunting entitled,
Old and most excellent 'mong all of the treasures;
Its blade was of iron, blotted with poison,
Hardened with gore; it failed not in battle
75
Any hero under heaven in hand who it brandished,

Who ventured to take the terrible journeys,
The battle-field sought; not the earliest occasion
That deeds of daring 'twas destined to 'complish.
Unferth has little use for swords.
Ecglaf's kinsman minded not soothly,
80
Exulting in strength, what erst he had spoken
Drunken with wine, when the weapon he lent to
A sword-hero bolder; himself did not venture
'Neath the strife of the currents his life to endanger,
[51]
To fame-deeds perform; there he forfeited glory,
85
Repute for his strength. Not so with the other
When he clad in his corslet had equipped him for battle.
XXIII.
BEOWULF'S FIGHT WITH GRENDEL'S MOTHER.

Beowulf makes a parting speech to Hrothgar.
Beowulf spake, Ecgtheow's son:
"Recall now, oh, famous kinsman of Healfdene,
Prince very prudent, now to part I am ready,
Gold-friend of earlmen, what erst we agreed on,
If I fail, act as a kind liegelord to my thanes,5
Should I lay down my life in lending thee assistance,
When my earth-joys were over, thou wouldst evermore serve me
In stead of a father; my faithful thanemen,
My trusty retainers, protect thou and care for,
Fall I in battle: and, Hrothgar belovèd,
and send Higelac the jewels thou hast given me10
Send unto Higelac the high-valued jewels
Thou to me hast allotted. The lord of the Geatmen
May perceive from the gold, the Hrethling may see it
I should like my king to know how generous a lord I found thee to be.
When he looks on the jewels, that a gem-giver found I
Good over-measure, enjoyed him while able.
15
And the ancient heirloom Unferth permit thou,
The famed one to have, the heavy-sword splendid1
The hard-edgèd weapon; with Hrunting to aid me,
I shall gain me glory, or grim-death shall take me."
Beowulf is eager for the fray.
The atheling of Geatmen uttered these words and
20
Heroic did hasten, not any rejoinder

Was willing to wait for; the wave-current swallowed
He is a whole day reaching the bottom of the sea.
The doughty-in-battle. Then a day's-length elapsed ere
He was able to see the sea at its bottom.
Early she found then who fifty of winters
25
The course of the currents kept in her fury,
Grisly and greedy, that the grim one's dominion
[52]Grendel's mother knows that some one has reached her domains.
Some one of men from above was exploring.
Forth did she grab them, grappled the warrior
With horrible clutches; yet no sooner she injured
30
His body unscathèd: the burnie out-guarded,
That she proved but powerless to pierce through the armor,
The limb-mail locked, with loath-grabbing fingers.
The sea-wolf bare then, when bottomward came she,
She grabs him, and bears him to her den.
The ring-prince homeward, that he after was powerless
35
(He had daring to do it) to deal with his weapons,
But many a mere-beast tormented him swimming,
Sea-monsters bite and strike him.
Flood-beasts no few with fierce-biting tusks did
Break through his burnie, the brave one pursued they.
The earl then discovered he was down in some cavern
40
Where no water whatever anywise harmed him,
And the clutch of the current could come not anear him,
Since the roofed-hall prevented; brightness a-gleaming
Fire-light he saw, flashing resplendent.
The good one saw then the sea-bottom's monster,
Beowulf attacks the mother of Grendel.45
The mighty mere-woman; he made a great onset
With weapon-of-battle, his hand not desisted
From striking, that war-blade struck on her head then
A battle-song greedy. The stranger perceived then
The sword will not bite.
The sword would not bite, her life would not injure,
50
But the falchion failed the folk-prince when straitened:
Erst had it often onsets encountered,
Oft cloven the helmet, the fated one's armor:
'Twas the first time that ever the excellent jewel
Had failed of its fame. Firm-mooded after,

55

Not heedless of valor, but mindful of glory,
Was Higelac's kinsman; the hero-chief angry
Cast then his carved-sword covered with jewels
That it lay on the earth, hard and steel-pointed;
The hero throws down all weapons, and again trusts to his hand-grip.
He hoped in his strength, his hand-grapple sturdy.

60

So any must act whenever he thinketh
To gain him in battle glory unending,
And is reckless of living. The lord of the War-Geats
[53]
(He shrank not from battle) seized by the shoulder2
The mother of Grendel; then mighty in struggle

65

Swung he his enemy, since his anger was kindled,
That she fell to the floor. With furious grapple
Beowulf falls.
She gave him requital3 early thereafter,
And stretched out to grab him; the strongest of warriors
Faint-mooded stumbled, till he fell in his traces,
The monster sits on him with drawn sword.70
Foot-going champion. Then she sat on the hall-guest
And wielded her war-knife wide-bladed, flashing,
For her son would take vengeance, her one only bairn.
His armor saves his life.
His breast-armor woven bode on his shoulder;
It guarded his life, the entrance defended

75

'Gainst sword-point and edges. Ecgtheow's son there
Had fatally journeyed, champion of Geatmen,
In the arms of the ocean, had the armor not given,
Close-woven corslet, comfort and succor,
God arranged for his escape.
And had God most holy not awarded the victory,

80

All-knowing Lord; easily did heaven's
Ruler most righteous arrange it with justice;4
Uprose he erect ready for battle.

[1] Kl. emends 'wæl-sweord.' The half-line would then read, 'the battle-sword splendid.'—For 'heard-ecg' in next half-verse, see note to 20 39 above.
[2] Sw., R., and t.B. suggest 'feaxe' for 'eaxle' (1538) and render: Seized by the hair.
[3] If 'hand-léan' be accepted (as the MS. has it), the line will read: She hand-reward gave him early thereafter.

93

[4] Sw. and S. change H.-So.'s semicolon (v. 1557) to a comma, and translate: The Ruler of Heaven arranged it in justice easily, after he arose again.

XXIV.

BEOWULF IS DOUBLE-CONQUEROR.

Beowulf grasps a giant-sword,
Then he saw mid the war-gems a weapon of victory,
An ancient giant-sword, of edges a-doughty,
Glory of warriors: of weapons 'twas choicest,
Only 'twas larger than any man else was
[54]5
Able to bear to the battle-encounter,
The good and splendid work of the giants.
He grasped then the sword-hilt, knight of the Scyldings,
Bold and battle-grim, brandished his ring-sword,
Hopeless of living, hotly he smote her,
10
That the fiend-woman's neck firmly it grappled,
and fells the female monster.
Broke through her bone-joints, the bill fully pierced her
Fate-cursèd body, she fell to the ground then:
The hand-sword was bloody, the hero exulted.
The brand was brilliant, brightly it glimmered,
15
Just as from heaven gemlike shineth
The torch of the firmament. He glanced 'long the building,
And turned by the wall then, Higelac's vassal
Raging and wrathful raised his battle-sword
Strong by the handle. The edge was not useless
20
To the hero-in-battle, but he speedily wished to
Give Grendel requital for the many assaults he
Had worked on the West-Danes not once, but often,
When he slew in slumber the subjects of Hrothgar,
Swallowed down fifteen sleeping retainers
25
Of the folk of the Danemen, and fully as many
Carried away, a horrible prey.
He gave him requital, grim-raging champion,
Beowulf sees the body of Grendel, and cuts off his head.
When he saw on his rest-place weary of conflict
Grendel lying, of life-joys bereavèd,
30
As the battle at Heorot erstwhile had scathed him;
His body far bounded, a blow when he suffered,

Death having seized him, sword-smiting heavy,
And he cut off his head then. Early this noticed
The clever carles who as comrades of Hrothgar
The waters are gory.35
Gazed on the sea-deeps, that the surging wave-currents
Were mightily mingled, the mere-flood was gory:
Of the good one the gray-haired together held converse,
Beowulf is given up for dead.
The hoary of head, that they hoped not to see again
The atheling ever, that exulting in victory
40
He'd return there to visit the distinguished folk-ruler:
[55]
Then many concluded the mere-wolf had killed him.1
The ninth hour came then. From the ness-edge departed
The bold-mooded Scyldings; the gold-friend of heroes
Homeward betook him. The strangers sat down then
45
Soul-sick, sorrowful, the sea-waves regarding:
They wished and yet weened not their well-loved friend-lord
The giant-sword melts.
To see any more. The sword-blade began then,
The blood having touched it, contracting and shriveling
With battle-icicles; 'twas a wonderful marvel
50
That it melted entirely, likest to ice when
The Father unbindeth the bond of the frost and
Unwindeth the wave-bands, He who wieldeth dominion
Of times and of tides: a truth-firm Creator.
Nor took he of jewels more in the dwelling,
55
Lord of the Weders, though they lay all around him,
Than the head and the handle handsome with jewels;
[56]
The brand early melted, burnt was the weapon:2
So hot was the blood, the strange-spirit poisonous
The hero swims back to the realms of day.
That in it did perish. He early swam off then
60
Who had bided in combat the carnage of haters,
Went up through the ocean; the eddies were cleansèd,

The spacious expanses, when the spirit from farland
His life put aside and this short-lived existence.
The seamen's defender came swimming to land then
65
Doughty of spirit, rejoiced in his sea-gift,
The bulky burden which he bore in his keeping.
The excellent vassals advanced then to meet him,
To God they were grateful, were glad in their chieftain,
That to see him safe and sound was granted them.
70
From the high-minded hero, then, helmet and burnie
Were speedily loosened: the ocean was putrid,
The water 'neath welkin weltered with gore.
Forth did they fare, then, their footsteps retracing,
Merry and mirthful, measured the earth-way,
75
The highway familiar: men very daring3
Bare then the head from the sea-cliff, burdening
Each of the earlmen, excellent-valiant.
It takes four men to carry Grendel's head on a spear.
Four of them had to carry with labor
The head of Grendel to the high towering gold-hall
80
Upstuck on the spear, till fourteen most-valiant
And battle-brave Geatmen came there going
Straight to the palace: the prince of the people
Measured the mead-ways, their mood-brave companion.

The atheling of earlmen entered the building,
85
Deed-valiant man, adorned with distinction,
Doughty shield-warrior, to address King Hrothgar:
[57]
Then hung by the hair, the head of Grendel
Was borne to the building, where beer-thanes were drinking,
Loth before earlmen and eke 'fore the lady:
90
The warriors beheld then a wonderful sight.

[1] 'Þæs monige gewearð' (1599) and 'hafað þæs geworden' (2027).—In a paper published some years ago in one of the Johns Hopkins University circulars, I tried to throw upon these two long-doubtful passages some light derived from a study of like passages in Alfred's prose.—The impersonal verb 'geweorðan,' with an accus. of the person, and a þæt-clause is used several times with the meaning 'agree.' See Orosius (Sweet's ed.) 1787; 20434; 20828; 21015; 28020. In the two Beowulf passages, the þæt-clause is anticipated by 'þæs,' which is clearly a gen. of the thing agreed on.

The first passage (v. 1599 (b)-1600) I translate literally: Then many agreed upon this (namely), that the sea-wolf had killed him.

The second passage (v. 2025 (b)-2027): She is promised …; to this the friend of the Scyldings has agreed, etc. By emending 'is' instead of 'wæs' (2025), the tenses will be brought into perfect harmony.

In v. 1997 ff. this same idiom occurs, and was noticed in B.'s great article on Beowulf, which appeared about the time I published my reading of 1599 and 2027. Translate 1997 then: Wouldst let the South-Danes themselves decide about their struggle with Grendel. Here 'Súð-Dene' is accus. of person, and 'gúðe' is gen. of thing agreed on.

With such collateral support as that afforded by B. (P. and B. XII. 97), I have no hesitation in departing from H.-So., my usual guide.

The idiom above treated runs through A.-S., Old Saxon, and other Teutonic languages, and should be noticed in the lexicons.

[2] 'Bróden-mæl' is regarded by most scholars as meaning a damaskeened sword. Translate: The damaskeened sword burned up. Cf. 25 16 and note.

[3] 'Cyning-balde' (1635) is the much-disputed reading of K. and Th. To render this, "nobly bold," "excellently bold," have been suggested. B. would read 'cyning-holde' (cf. 290), and render: Men well-disposed towards the king carried the head, etc. 'Cynebealde,' says t.B., endorsing Gr.

XXV.
BEOWULF BRINGS HIS TROPHIES.—HROTHGAR'S GRATITUDE.

Beowulf relates his last exploit.
Beowulf spake, offspring of Ecgtheow:
"Lo! we blithely have brought thee, bairn of Healfdene,
Prince of the Scyldings, these presents from ocean

97

Which thine eye looketh on, for an emblem of glory.
5
I came off alive from this, narrowly 'scaping:
In war 'neath the water the work with great pains I
Performed, and the fight had been finished quite nearly,
Had God not defended me. I failed in the battle
Aught to accomplish, aided by Hrunting,
10
Though that weapon was worthy, but the Wielder of earth-folk
God was fighting with me.
Gave me willingly to see on the wall a
Heavy old hand-sword hanging in splendor
(He guided most often the lorn and the friendless),
That I swung as a weapon. The wards of the house then
15
I killed in the conflict (when occasion was given me).
Then the battle-sword burned, the brand that was lifted,1
As the blood-current sprang, hottest of war-sweats;
Seizing the hilt, from my foes I offbore it;
I avenged as I ought to their acts of malignity,
20
The murder of Danemen. I then make thee this promise,
Heorot is freed from monsters.
Thou'lt be able in Heorot careless to slumber
With thy throng of heroes and the thanes of thy people
Every and each, of greater and lesser,
And thou needest not fear for them from the selfsame direction
25
As thou formerly fearedst, oh, folk-lord of Scyldings,
[58]
End-day for earlmen." To the age-hoary man then,
The famous sword is presented to Hrothgar.
The gray-haired chieftain, the gold-fashioned sword-hilt,
Old-work of giants, was thereupon given;
Since the fall of the fiends, it fell to the keeping
30
Of the wielder of Danemen, the wonder-smith's labor,
And the bad-mooded being abandoned this world then,
Opponent of God, victim of murder,
And also his mother; it went to the keeping
Of the best of the world-kings, where waters encircle,
35
Who the scot divided in Scylding dominion.
Hrothgar looks closely at the old sword.
Hrothgar discoursed, the hilt he regarded,

The ancient heirloom where an old-time contention's
Beginning was graven: the gurgling currents,
The flood slew thereafter the race of the giants,
40
They had proved themselves daring: that people was loth to
It had belonged to a race hateful to God.
The Lord everlasting, through lash of the billows
The Father gave them final requital.
So in letters of rune on the clasp of the handle
Gleaming and golden, 'twas graven exactly,
45
Set forth and said, whom that sword had been made for,
Finest of irons, who first it was wrought for,
Wreathed at its handle and gleaming with serpents.
The wise one then said (silent they all were)
Hrothgar praises Beowulf.
Son of old Healfdene: "He may say unrefuted
50
Who performs 'mid the folk-men fairness and truth
(The hoary old ruler remembers the past),
That better by birth is this bairn of the nobles!
Thy fame is extended through far-away countries,
Good friend Beowulf, o'er all of the races,
55
Thou holdest all firmly, hero-like strength with
Prudence of spirit. I'll prove myself grateful
As before we agreed on; thou granted for long shalt
Become a great comfort to kinsmen and comrades,
Heremod's career is again contrasted with Beowulf's.
A help unto heroes. Heremod became not
60
Such to the Scyldings, successors of Ecgwela;
He grew not to please them, but grievous destruction,
[59]
And diresome death-woes to Danemen attracted;
He slew in anger his table-companions,
Trustworthy counsellors, till he turned off lonely
65
From world-joys away, wide-famous ruler:
Though high-ruling heaven in hero-strength raised him,
In might exalted him, o'er men of all nations
Made him supreme, yet a murderous spirit
Grew in his bosom: he gave then no ring-gems
*A wretched failure of a king, to give no jewels to his retainers.*70
To the Danes after custom; endured he unjoyful

99

Standing the straits from strife that was raging,
Longsome folk-sorrow. Learn then from this,
Lay hold of virtue! Though laden with winters,
I have sung thee these measures. 'Tis a marvel to tell it,
Hrothgar moralizes.75
How all-ruling God from greatness of spirit
Giveth wisdom to children of men,
Manor and earlship: all things He ruleth.
He often permitteth the mood-thought of man of
The illustrious lineage to lean to possessions,
80
Allows him earthly delights at his manor,
A high-burg of heroes to hold in his keeping,
Maketh portions of earth-folk hear him,
And a wide-reaching kingdom so that, wisdom failing him,
He himself is unable to reckon its boundaries;
85
He liveth in luxury, little debars him,
Nor sickness nor age, no treachery-sorrow
Becloudeth his spirit, conflict nowhere,
No sword-hate, appeareth, but all of the world doth
Wend as he wisheth; the worse he knoweth not,
90
Till arrant arrogance inward pervading,
Waxeth and springeth, when the warder is sleeping,
The guard of the soul: with sorrows encompassed,
Too sound is his slumber, the slayer is near him,
Who with bow and arrow aimeth in malice.
[60]
[1] Or rather, perhaps, 'the inlaid, or damaskeened weapon.' Cf. 24 57 and note.
XXVI.
HROTHGAR MORALIZES.—REST AFTER LABOR.

A wounded spirit.
"Then bruised in his bosom he with bitter-toothed missile
Is hurt 'neath his helmet: from harmful pollution
He is powerless to shield him by the wonderful mandates
Of the loath-cursèd spirit; what too long he hath holden
5
Him seemeth too small, savage he hoardeth,
Nor boastfully giveth gold-plated rings,1
The fate of the future flouts and forgetteth
Since God had erst given him greatness no little,
Wielder of Glory. His end-day anear,
10
It afterward happens that the bodily-dwelling
Fleetingly fadeth, falls into ruins;
Another lays hold who doleth the ornaments,
The nobleman's jewels, nothing lamenting,
Heedeth no terror. Oh, Beowulf dear,
15
Best of the heroes, from bale-strife defend thee,
And choose thee the better, counsels eternal;
Be not over proud: life is fleeting, and its strength soon wasteth away.
Beware of arrogance, world-famous champion!
But a little-while lasts thy life-vigor's fulness;
'Twill after hap early, that illness or sword-edge
20

Shall part thee from strength, or the grasp of the fire,
Or the wave of the current, or clutch of the edges,
Or flight of the war-spear, or age with its horrors,
Or thine eyes' bright flashing shall fade into darkness:
'Twill happen full early, excellent hero,
Hrothgar gives an account of his reign.25
That death shall subdue thee. So the Danes a half-century
I held under heaven, helped them in struggles
'Gainst many a race in middle-earth's regions,
With ash-wood and edges, that enemies none
On earth molested me. Lo! offsetting change, now,
[61]Sorrow after joy.30
Came to my manor, grief after joyance,
When Grendel became my constant visitor,
Inveterate hater: I from that malice
Continually travailed with trouble no little.
Thanks be to God that I gained in my lifetime,
35
To the Lord everlasting, to look on the gory
Head with mine eyes, after long-lasting sorrow!
Go to the bench now, battle-adornèd
Joy in the feasting: of jewels in common
We'll meet with many when morning appeareth."
40
The Geatman was gladsome, ganged he immediately
To go to the bench, as the clever one bade him.
Then again as before were the famous-for-prowess,
Hall-inhabiters, handsomely banqueted,
Feasted anew. The night-veil fell then
45
Dark o'er the warriors. The courtiers rose then;
The gray-haired was anxious to go to his slumbers,
The hoary old Scylding. Hankered the Geatman,
Beowulf is fagged, and seeks rest.
The champion doughty, greatly, to rest him:
An earlman early outward did lead him,
50
Fagged from his faring, from far-country springing,
Who for etiquette's sake all of a liegeman's
Needs regarded, such as seamen at that time
Were bounden to feel. The big-hearted rested;
The building uptowered, spacious and gilded,
55
The guest within slumbered, till the sable-clad raven
Blithely foreboded the beacon of heaven.

Then the bright-shining sun o'er the bottoms came going;2
The warriors hastened, the heads of the peoples
Were ready to go again to their peoples,
The Geats prepare to leave Dane-land.60
The high-mooded farer would faraway thenceward
Look for his vessel. The valiant one bade then,3
[62]Unferth asks Beowulf to accept his sword as a gift. Beowulf thanks him.
Offspring of Ecglaf, off to bear Hrunting,
To take his weapon, his well-beloved iron;
He him thanked for the gift, saying good he accounted
65
The war-friend and mighty, nor chid he with words then
The blade of the brand: 'twas a brave-mooded hero.
When the warriors were ready, arrayed in their trappings,
The atheling dear to the Danemen advanced then
On to the dais, where the other was sitting,
70
Grim-mooded hero, greeted King Hrothgar.
[1] K. says 'proudly giveth.'—Gr. says, 'And gives no gold-plated rings, in order
to incite the recipient to boastfulness.'—B. suggests 'gyld' for 'gylp,' and renders:
And gives no beaten rings for reward.
[2] If S.'s emendation be accepted, v. 57 will read: Then came the light, going
bright after darkness: the warriors, etc.
[3] As the passage stands in H.-So., Unferth presents Beowulf with the sword
Hrunting, and B. thanks him for the gift. If, however, the suggestions of Grdtvg.
and M. be accepted, the passage will read: Then the brave one (i.e. Beowulf)
commanded that Hrunting be borne to the son of Ecglaf (Unferth), bade him take
his sword, his dear weapon; he (B.) thanked him (U.) for the loan, etc.
XXVII.
SORROW AT PARTING.

Beowulf's farewell.
Beowulf spake, Ecgtheow's offspring:
"We men of the water wish to declare now
Fared from far-lands, we're firmly determined
To seek King Higelac. Here have we fitly
5
Been welcomed and feasted, as heart would desire it;
Good was the greeting. If greater affection
I am anywise able ever on earth to
Gain at thy hands, ruler of heroes,
Than yet I have done, I shall quickly be ready
I shall be ever ready to aid thee.10
For combat and conflict. O'er the course of the waters
Learn I that neighbors alarm thee with terror,

As haters did whilom, I hither will bring thee
For help unto heroes henchmen by thousands.
My liegelord will encourage me in aiding thee.
I know as to Higelac, the lord of the Geatmen,
15
Though young in years, he yet will permit me,
By words and by works, ward of the people,
Fully to furnish thee forces and bear thee
My lance to relieve thee, if liegemen shall fail thee,
And help of my hand-strength; if Hrethric be treating,
[63]20
Bairn of the king, at the court of the Geatmen,
He thereat may find him friends in abundance:
Faraway countries he were better to seek for
Who trusts in himself." Hrothgar discoursed then,
Making rejoinder: "These words thou hast uttered
25
All-knowing God hath given thy spirit!
O Beowulf, thou art wise beyond thy years.
Ne'er heard I an earlman thus early in life
More clever in speaking: thou'rt cautious of spirit,
Mighty of muscle, in mouth-answers prudent.
I count on the hope that, happen it ever
30
That missile shall rob thee of Hrethel's descendant,
Edge-horrid battle, and illness or weapon
Deprive thee of prince, of people's protector,
Should Higelac die, the Geats could find no better successor than thou wouldst
make.
And life thou yet holdest, the Sea-Geats will never
Find a more fitting folk-lord to choose them,
35
Gem-ward of heroes, than thou mightest prove thee,
If the kingdom of kinsmen thou carest to govern.
Thy mood-spirit likes me the longer the better,
Beowulf dear: thou hast brought it to pass that
To both these peoples peace shall be common,
Thou hast healed the ancient breach between our races.40
To Geat-folk and Danemen, the strife be suspended,
The secret assailings they suffered in yore-days;
And also that jewels be shared while I govern
The wide-stretching kingdom, and that many shall visit
Others o'er the ocean with excellent gift-gems:
45
The ring-adorned bark shall bring o'er the currents

Presents and love-gifts. This people I know
Tow'rd foeman and friend firmly established,1
After ancient etiquette everywise blameless."
Then the warden of earlmen gave him still farther,
Parting gifts50
Kinsman of Healfdene, a dozen of jewels,
Bade him safely seek with the presents
His well-beloved people, early returning.
[64]Hrothgar kisses Beowulf, and weeps.
Then the noble-born king kissed the distinguished,
Dear-lovèd liegeman, the Dane-prince saluted him,
55
And claspèd his neck; tears from him fell,
From the gray-headed man: he two things expected,
Agèd and reverend, but rather the second,
2That bold in council they'd meet thereafter.
The man was so dear that he failed to suppress the
60
Emotions that moved him, but in mood-fetters fastened
The old king is deeply grieved to part with his benefactor.
The long-famous hero longeth in secret
Deep in his spirit for the dear-beloved man
Though not a blood-kinsman. Beowulf thenceward,
Gold-splendid warrior, walked o'er the meadows
65
Exulting in treasure: the sea-going vessel
Riding at anchor awaited its owner.
As they pressed on their way then, the present of Hrothgar
Giving liberally is the true proof of kingship.
Was frequently referred to: a folk-king indeed that
Everyway blameless, till age did debar him
70
The joys of his might, which hath many oft injured.
[1] For 'geworhte,' the crux of this passage, B. proposes 'geþóhte,' rendering: I know this people with firm thought every way blameless towards foe and friends.
[2] S. and B. emend so as to negative the verb 'meet.' "Why should Hrothgar weep if he expects to meet Beowulf again?" both these scholars ask. But the weeping is mentioned before the 'expectations': the tears may have been due to many emotions, especially gratitude, struggling for expression.
XXVIII.
THE HOMEWARD JOURNEY.—THE TWO QUEENS.

105

Then the band of very valiant retainers
Came to the current; they were clad all in armor,
The coast-guard again.
In link-woven burnies. The land-warder noticed
The return of the earlmen, as he erstwhile had seen them;
5
Nowise with insult he greeted the strangers
From the naze of the cliff, but rode on to meet them;
Said the bright-armored visitors1 vesselward traveled
[65]
Welcome to Weders. The wide-bosomed craft then
Lay on the sand, laden with armor,
10
With horses and jewels, the ring-stemmèd sailer:
The mast uptowered o'er the treasure of Hrothgar.
Beowulf gives the guard a handsome sword.
To the boat-ward a gold-bound brand he presented,
That he was afterwards honored on the ale-bench more highly
As the heirloom's owner. 2Set he out on his vessel,
15
To drive on the deep, Dane-country left he.
Along by the mast then a sea-garment fluttered,
A rope-fastened sail. The sea-boat resounded,
The wind o'er the waters the wave-floater nowise

Kept from its journey; the sea-goer traveled,
20
The foamy-necked floated forth o'er the currents,
The well-fashioned vessel o'er the ways of the ocean,
The Geats see their own land again.
Till they came within sight of the cliffs of the Geatmen,
The well-known headlands. The wave-goer hastened
Driven by breezes, stood on the shore.
The port-warden is anxiously looking for them.25
Prompt at the ocean, the port-ward was ready,
Who long in the past outlooked in the distance,3
At water's-edge waiting well-lovèd heroes;
He bound to the bank then the broad-bosomed vessel
Fast in its fetters, lest the force of the waters
30
Should be able to injure the ocean-wood winsome.
Bade he up then take the treasure of princes,
Plate-gold and fretwork; not far was it thence
To go off in search of the giver of jewels:
[66]
Hrethel's son Higelac at home there remaineth,4
35
Himself with his comrades close to the sea-coast.
The building was splendid, the king heroic,
Great in his hall, Hygd very young was,
Hygd, the noble queen of Higelac, lavish of gifts.
Fine-mooded, clever, though few were the winters
That the daughter of Hæreth had dwelt in the borough;
40
But she nowise was cringing nor niggard of presents,
Of ornaments rare, to the race of the Geatmen.
Offa's consort, Thrytho, is contrasted with Hygd.
Thrytho nursed anger, excellent5 folk-queen,
Hot-burning hatred: no hero whatever
'Mong household companions, her husband excepted
She is a terror to all save her husband.45
Dared to adventure to look at the woman
With eyes in the daytime;6 but he knew that death-chains
Hand-wreathed were wrought him: early thereafter,
When the hand-strife was over, edges were ready,
That fierce-raging sword-point had to force a decision,
50
Murder-bale show. Such no womanly custom
For a lady to practise, though lovely her person,
That a weaver-of-peace, on pretence of anger

107

A belovèd liegeman of life should deprive.
Soothly this hindered Heming's kinsman;
55
Other ale-drinking earlmen asserted
That fearful folk-sorrows fewer she wrought them,
Treacherous doings, since first she was given
Adorned with gold to the war-hero youthful,
For her origin honored, when Offa's great palace
60
O'er the fallow flood by her father's instructions
She sought on her journey, where she afterwards fully,
Famed for her virtue, her fate on the king's-seat
[67]
Enjoyed in her lifetime, love did she hold with
The ruler of heroes, the best, it is told me,
65
Of all of the earthmen that oceans encompass,
Of earl-kindreds endless; hence Offa was famous
Far and widely, by gifts and by battles,
Spear-valiant hero; the home of his fathers
He governed with wisdom, whence Eomær did issue
70
For help unto heroes, Heming's kinsman,
Grandson of Garmund, great in encounters.

[1] For 'scawan' (1896), 'scaðan' has been proposed. Accepting this, we may render: He said the bright-armored warriors were going to their vessel, welcome, etc. (Cf. 1804.)

[2] R. suggests, 'Gewát him on naca,' and renders: The vessel set out, to drive on the sea, the Dane-country left. 'On' bears the alliteration; cf. 'on hafu' (2524). This has some advantages over the H.-So. reading; viz. (1) It adds nothing to the text; (2) it makes 'naca' the subject, and thus brings the passage into keeping with the context, where the poet has exhausted his vocabulary in detailing the actions of the vessel.—B.'s emendation (cf. P. and B. XII. 97) is violent.

[3] B. translates: Who for a long time, ready at the coast, had looked out into the distance eagerly for the dear men. This changes the syntax of 'léofra manna.'

[4] For 'wunað' (v. 1924) several eminent critics suggest 'wunade' (=remained). This makes the passage much clearer.

[5] Why should such a woman be described as an 'excellent' queen? C. suggests 'frécnu' = dangerous, bold.

[6] For 'an dæges' various readings have been offered. If 'and-éges' be accepted, the sentence will read: No hero ... dared look upon her, eye to eye. If 'án-dæges' be adopted, translate: Dared look upon her the whole day.

XXIX.

BEOWULF AND HIGELAC.

Then the brave one departed, his band along with him,
Beowulf and his party seek Higelac.
Seeking the sea-shore, the sea-marches treading,
The wide-stretching shores. The world-candle glimmered,
The sun from the southward; they proceeded then onward,
5
Early arriving where they heard that the troop-lord,
Ongentheow's slayer, excellent, youthful
Folk-prince and warrior was distributing jewels,
Close in his castle. The coming of Beowulf
Was announced in a message quickly to Higelac,
10
That the folk-troop's defender forth to the palace
The linden-companion alive was advancing,
Secure from the combat courtward a-going.
The building was early inward made ready
For the foot-going guests as the good one had ordered.
Beowulf sits by his liegelord.15
He sat by the man then who had lived through the struggle,
Kinsman by kinsman, when the king of the people
Had in lordly language saluted the dear one,
Queen Hygd receives the heroes.
In words that were formal. The daughter of Hæreth
Coursed through the building, carrying mead-cups:1
[68]20
She loved the retainers, tendered the beakers
To the high-minded Geatmen. Higelac 'gan then
Higelac is greatly interested in Beowulf's adventures.
Pleasantly plying his companion with questions
In the high-towering palace. A curious interest
Tormented his spirit, what meaning to see in
25
The Sea-Geats' adventures: "Beowulf worthy,
Give an account of thy adventures, Beowulf dear.
How throve your journeying, when thou thoughtest suddenly
Far o'er the salt-streams to seek an encounter,
A battle at Heorot? Hast bettered for Hrothgar,
The famous folk-leader, his far-published sorrows
30
Any at all? In agony-billows
My suspense has been great.
I mused upon torture, distrusted the journey
Of the belovèd liegeman; I long time did pray thee
By no means to seek out the murderous spirit,
To suffer the South-Danes themselves to decide on2

35
Grappling with Grendel. To God I am thankful
To be suffered to see thee safe from thy journey."
Beowulf narrates his adventures.
Beowulf answered, bairn of old Ecgtheow:
"'Tis hidden by no means, Higelac chieftain,
From many of men, the meeting so famous,
40
What mournful moments of me and of Grendel
Were passed in the place where he pressing affliction
On the Victory-Scyldings scathefully brought,
Anguish forever; that all I avengèd,
So that any under heaven of the kinsmen of Grendel
Grendel's kindred have no cause to boast.45
Needeth not boast of that cry-in-the-morning,
Who longest liveth of the loth-going kindred,3
Encompassed by moorland. I came in my journey
To the royal ring-hall, Hrothgar to greet there:
Hrothgar received me very cordially.
Soon did the famous scion of Healfdene,
50
When he understood fully the spirit that led me,
Assign me a seat with the son of his bosom.
[69]
The troop was in joyance; mead-glee greater
'Neath arch of the ether not ever beheld I
The queen also showed up no little honor.
'Mid hall-building holders. The highly-famed queen,
55
Peace-tie of peoples, oft passed through the building,
Cheered the young troopers; she oft tendered a hero
A beautiful ring-band, ere she went to her sitting.
Hrothgar's lovely daughter.
Oft the daughter of Hrothgar in view of the courtiers
To the earls at the end the ale-vessel carried,
60
Whom Freaware I heard then hall-sitters title,
When nail-adorned jewels she gave to the heroes:
She is betrothed to Ingeld, in order to unite the Danes and Heathobards.
Gold-bedecked, youthful, to the glad son of Froda
Her faith has been plighted; the friend of the Scyldings,
The guard of the kingdom, hath given his sanction,4
65
And counts it a vantage, for a part of the quarrels,
A portion of hatred, to pay with the woman.

5Somewhere not rarely, when the ruler has fallen,
The life-taking lance relaxeth its fury
For a brief breathing-spell, though the bride be charming!
[1] 'Meodu-scencum' (1981) some would render 'with mead-pourers.' Translate
then: The daughter of Hæreth went through the building accompanied by mead-
pourers.
[2] See my note to 1599, supra, and B. in P. and B. XII. 97.
[3] For 'fenne,' supplied by Grdtvg., B. suggests 'fácne' (cf. Jul. 350). Accepting
this, translate: Who longest lives of the hated race, steeped in treachery.
[4] See note to v. 1599 above.
[5] This is perhaps the least understood sentence in the poem, almost every word
being open to dispute. (1) The 'nó' of our text is an emendation, and is rejected by
many scholars. (2) 'Seldan' is by some taken as an adv. (= seldom), and by others
as a noun (= page, companion). (3) 'Léod-hryre,' some render 'fall of the people';
others, 'fall of the prince.' (4) 'Búgeð,' most scholars regard as the intrans. verb
meaning 'bend,' 'rest'; but one great scholar has translated it 'shall kill.' (5)
'Hwær,' Very recently, has been attacked, 'wære' being suggested. (6) As a
corollary to the above, the same critic proposes to drop 'oft' out of the text.—t.B.
suggests: Oft seldan wære after léodhryre: lýtle hwíle bongár búgeð, þéah séo
brýd duge = often has a treaty been (thus) struck, after a prince had fallen: (but
only) a short time is the spear (then) wont to rest, however excellent the bride may
be.
XXX.
BEOWULF NARRATES HIS ADVENTURES TO HIGELAC.

"It well may discomfit the prince of the Heathobards
And each of the thanemen of earls that attend him,
[70]
When he goes to the building escorting the woman,
That a noble-born Daneman the knights should be feasting:
5
There gleam on his person the leavings of elders
Hard and ring-bright, Heathobards' treasure,
While they wielded their arms, till they misled to the battle
Their own dear lives and belovèd companions.
He saith at the banquet who the collar beholdeth,
10
An ancient ash-warrior who earlmen's destruction
Clearly recalleth (cruel his spirit),
Sadly beginneth sounding the youthful
Thane-champion's spirit through the thoughts of his bosom,
War-grief to waken, and this word-answer speaketh:
Ingeld is stirred up to break the truce.15
'Art thou able, my friend, to know when thou seest it
The brand which thy father bare to the conflict

111

In his latest adventure, 'neath visor of helmet,
The dearly-loved iron, where Danemen did slay him,
And brave-mooded Scyldings, on the fall of the heroes,
20
(When vengeance was sleeping) the slaughter-place wielded?
E'en now some man of the murderer's progeny
Exulting in ornaments enters the building,
Boasts of his blood-shedding, offbeareth the jewel
Which thou shouldst wholly hold in possession!'
25
So he urgeth and mindeth on every occasion
With woe-bringing words, till waxeth the season
When the woman's thane for the works of his father,
The bill having bitten, blood-gory sleepeth,
Fated to perish; the other one thenceward
30
'Scapeth alive, the land knoweth thoroughly.1
Then the oaths of the earlmen on each side are broken,
When rancors unresting are raging in Ingeld
And his wife-love waxeth less warm after sorrow.
So the Heathobards' favor not faithful I reckon,
35
Their part in the treaty not true to the Danemen,
Their friendship not fast. I further shall tell thee
[71]Having made these preliminary statements, I will now tell thee of Grendel, the monster.
More about Grendel, that thou fully mayst hear,
Ornament-giver, what afterward came from
The hand-rush of heroes. When heaven's bright jewel
40
O'er earthfields had glided, the stranger came raging,
The horrible night-fiend, us for to visit,
Where wholly unharmed the hall we were guarding.
Hondscio fell first
To Hondscio happened a hopeless contention,
Death to the doomed one, dead he fell foremost,
45
Girded war-champion; to him Grendel became then,
To the vassal distinguished, a tooth-weaponed murderer,
The well-beloved henchman's body all swallowed.
Not the earlier off empty of hand did
The bloody-toothed murderer, mindful of evils,
50
Wish to escape from the gold-giver's palace,
But sturdy of strength he strove to outdo me,

Hand-ready grappled. A glove was suspended
Spacious and wondrous, in art-fetters fastened,
Which was fashioned entirely by touch of the craftman
55
From the dragon's skin by the devil's devices:
He down in its depths would do me unsadly
One among many, deed-doer raging,
Though sinless he saw me; not so could it happen
When I in my anger upright did stand.
60

'Tis too long to recount how requital I furnished
For every evil to the earlmen's destroyer;
I reflected honor upon my people.
'Twas there, my prince, that I proudly distinguished
Thy land with my labors. He left and retreated,
He lived his life a little while longer:
65
Yet his right-hand guarded his footstep in Heorot,
And sad-mooded thence to the sea-bottom fell he,
Mournful in mind. For the might-rush of battle
King Hrothgar lavished gifts upon me.
The friend of the Scyldings, with gold that was plated,
With ornaments many, much requited me,
70
When daylight had dawned, and down to the banquet
We had sat us together. There was chanting and joyance:
The age-stricken Scylding asked many questions

And of old-times related; oft light-ringing harp-strings,
Joy-telling wood, were touched by the brave one;
75
Now he uttered measures, mourning and truthful,
Then the large-hearted land-king a legend of wonder
Truthfully told us. Now troubled with years
The old king is sad over the loss of his youthful vigor.
The age-hoary warrior afterward began to
Mourn for the might that marked him in youth-days;
80
His breast within boiled, when burdened with winters
Much he remembered. From morning till night then
We joyed us therein as etiquette suffered,
Till the second night season came unto earth-folk.
Then early thereafter, the mother of Grendel
Grendel's mother.85
Was ready for vengeance, wretched she journeyed;
Her son had death ravished, the wrath of the Geatmen.
The horrible woman avengèd her offspring,
And with mighty mainstrength murdered a hero.
Æschere falls a prey to her vengeance.
There the spirit of Æschere, agèd adviser,
90
Was ready to vanish; nor when morn had lightened
Were they anywise suffered to consume him with fire,
Folk of the Danemen, the death-weakened hero,
Nor the belovèd liegeman to lay on the pyre;
She suffered not his body to be burned, but ate it.
She the corpse had offcarried in the clutch of the foeman2
95
'Neath mountain-brook's flood. To Hrothgar 'twas saddest
Of pains that ever had preyed on the chieftain;
By the life of thee the land-prince then me3
Besought very sadly, in sea-currents' eddies
To display my prowess, to peril my safety,
100
Might-deeds accomplish; much did he promise.
I sought the creature in her den,
I found then the famous flood-current's cruel,
Horrible depth-warder. A while unto us two
Hand was in common; the currents were seething
With gore that was clotted, and Grendel's fierce mother's
and hewed her head off.105

Head I offhacked in the hall at the bottom
With huge-reaching sword-edge, hardly I wrested
My life from her clutches; not doomed was I then,
Jewels were freely bestowed upon me.
But the warden of earlmen afterward gave me
Jewels in quantity, kinsman of Healfdene.

[1] For 'lifigende' (2063), a mere conjecture, 'wígende' has been suggested. The line would then read: Escapeth by fighting, knows the land thoroughly.
[2] For 'fæðmum,' Gr.'s conjecture, B. proposes 'færunga.' These three half-verses would then read: She bore off the corpse of her foe suddenly under the mountain-torrent.
[3] The phrase 'þíne lýfe' (2132) was long rendered 'with thy (presupposed) permission.' The verse would read: The land-prince then sadly besought me, with thy (presupposed) permission, etc.

XXXI.
GIFT-GIVING IS MUTUAL.

"So the belovèd land-prince lived in decorum;
I had missed no rewards, no meeds of my prowess,
But he gave me jewels, regarding my wishes,
Healfdene his bairn; I'll bring them to thee, then,
All my gifts I lay at thy feet.5
Atheling of earlmen, offer them gladly.
And still unto thee is all my affection:1
But few of my folk-kin find I surviving
But thee, dear Higelac!" Bade he in then to carry2
The boar-image, banner, battle-high helmet,
10
Iron-gray armor, the excellent weapon,
This armor I have belonged of yore to Heregar.
In song-measures said: "This suit-for-the-battle
Hrothgar presented me, bade me expressly,
Wise-mooded atheling, thereafter to tell thee3
The whole of its history, said King Heregar owned it,
15
Dane-prince for long: yet he wished not to give then
[74]
The mail to his son, though dearly he loved him,
Hereward the hardy. Hold all in joyance!"
I heard that there followed hard on the jewels
Two braces of stallions of striking resemblance,
20
Dappled and yellow; he granted him usance
Of horses and treasures. So a kinsman should bear him,
No web of treachery weave for another,

Nor by cunning craftiness cause the destruction

Higelac loves his nephew Beowulf.

Of trusty companion. Most precious to Higelac,
25
The bold one in battle, was the bairn of his sister,
And each unto other mindful of favors.

Beowulf gives Hygd the necklace that Wealhtheow had given him.

I am told that to Hygd he proffered the necklace,
Wonder-gem rare that Wealhtheow gave him,
The troop-leader's daughter, a trio of horses
30
Slender and saddle-bright; soon did the jewel
Embellish her bosom, when the beer-feast was over.
So Ecgtheow's bairn brave did prove him,

Beowulf is famous.

War-famous man, by deeds that were valiant,
He lived in honor, belovèd companions
35
Slew not carousing; his mood was not cruel,
But by hand-strength hugest of heroes then living
The brave one retained the bountiful gift that
The Lord had allowed him. Long was he wretched,
So that sons of the Geatmen accounted him worthless,
40
And the lord of the liegemen loth was to do him
Mickle of honor, when mead-cups were passing;
They fully believed him idle and sluggish,

He is requited for the slights suffered in earlier days.

An indolent atheling: to the honor-blest man there
Came requital for the cuts he had suffered.
45
The folk-troop's defender bade fetch to the building
The heirloom of Hrethel, embellished with gold,

Higelac overwhelms the conqueror with gifts.

So the brave one enjoined it; there was jewel no richer
In the form of a weapon 'mong Geats of that era;
In Beowulf's keeping he placed it and gave him
50
Seven of thousands, manor and lordship.
Common to both was land 'mong the people,
[75]
Estate and inherited rights and possessions,
To the second one specially spacious dominions,
To the one who was better. It afterward happened
55

116

In days that followed, befell the battle-thanes,
After Heardred's death, Beowulf becomes king.
After Higelac's death, and when Heardred was murdered
With weapons of warfare 'neath well-covered targets,
When valiant battlemen in victor-band sought him,
War-Scylfing heroes harassed the nephew
60
Of Hereric in battle. To Beowulf's keeping
Turned there in time extensive dominions:
He rules the Geats fifty years.
He fittingly ruled them a fifty of winters
(He a man-ruler wise was, manor-ward old) till
A certain one 'gan, on gloom-darkening nights, a
The fire-drake.65
Dragon, to govern, who guarded a treasure,
A high-rising stone-cliff, on heath that was grayish:
A path 'neath it lay, unknown unto mortals.
Some one of earthmen entered the mountain,
The heathenish hoard laid hold of with ardor;
70

*   *   *   *   *   *   *
*   *   *   *   *   *   *
*   *   *   *   *   *   *
*   *   *   *   *   *   *
*   *   *   *   *   *   *

[1] This verse B. renders, 'Now serve I again thee alone as my gracious king.'
[2] For 'eafor' (2153), Kl. suggests 'ealdor.' Translate then: Bade the prince then to bear in the banner, battle-high helmet, etc. On the other hand, W. takes 'eaforhéafodsegn' as a compound, meaning 'helmet': He bade them bear in the helmet, battle-high helm, gray armor, etc.
[3] The H.-So. rendering (ærest = history, origin; 'eft' for 'est'), though liable to objection, is perhaps the best offered. 'That I should very early tell thee of his favor, kindness' sounds well; but 'his' is badly placed to limit 'ést.'—Perhaps, 'eft' with verbs of saying may have the force of Lat. prefix 're,' and the H.-So. reading mean, 'that I should its origin rehearse to thee.'
XXXII.
THE HOARD AND THE DRAGON.

*   *   *   *   *   *   *

He sought of himself who sorely did harm him,
But, for need very pressing, the servant of one of
The sons of the heroes hate-blows evaded,
5
Seeking for shelter and the sin-driven warrior
Took refuge within there. He early looked in it,

```
*       *       *       *       *       *       *
*       *       *       *       *       *       *
```
[76]
* * * * * when the onset surprised him,
The hoard.10
He a gem-vessel saw there: many of suchlike
Ancient ornaments in the earth-cave were lying,
As in days of yore some one of men of
Illustrious lineage, as a legacy monstrous,
There had secreted them, careful and thoughtful,
15
Dear-valued jewels. Death had offsnatched them,
In the days of the past, and the one man moreover
Of the flower of the folk who fared there the longest,
Was fain to defer it, friend-mourning warder,
A little longer to be left in enjoyment
20
Of long-lasting treasure.1 A barrow all-ready
Stood on the plain the stream-currents nigh to,
New by the ness-edge, unnethe of approaching:
The keeper of rings carried within a
2Ponderous deal of the treasure of nobles,
25
Of gold that was beaten, briefly he spake then:3
The ring-giver bewails the loss of retainers.
"Hold thou, O Earth, now heroes no more may,
The earnings of earlmen. Lo! erst in thy bosom
Worthy men won them; war-death hath ravished,
Perilous life-bale, all my warriors,
30
Liegemen belovèd, who this life have forsaken,
Who hall-pleasures saw. No sword-bearer have I,
And no one to burnish the gold-plated vessel,
The high-valued beaker: my heroes are vanished.
The hardy helmet behung with gilding
35
Shall be reaved of its riches: the ring-cleansers slumber
Who were charged to have ready visors-for-battle,
And the burnie that bided in battle-encounter
[77]
O'er breaking of war-shields the bite of the edges
Moulds with the hero. The ring-twisted armor,
40
Its lord being lifeless, no longer may journey
Hanging by heroes; harp-joy is vanished,

118

The rapture of glee-wood, no excellent falcon
Swoops through the building, no swift-footed charger
Grindeth the gravel. A grievous destruction
45
No few of the world-folk widely hath scattered!"
So, woful of spirit one after all
Lamented mournfully, moaning in sadness
By day and by night, till death with its billows
The fire-dragon
Dashed on his spirit. Then the ancient dusk-scather
50
Found the great treasure standing all open,
He who flaming and fiery flies to the barrows,
Naked war-dragon, nightly escapeth
Encompassed with fire; men under heaven
Widely beheld him. 'Tis said that he looks for4
55

The hoard in the earth, where old he is guarding
The heathenish treasure; he'll be nowise the better.
The dragon meets his match.
So three-hundred winters the waster of peoples
Held upon earth that excellent hoard-hall,
Till the forementioned earlman angered him bitterly:
60
The beat-plated beaker he bare to his chieftain
And fullest remission for all his remissness
Begged of his liegelord. Then the hoard5 was discovered,

The treasure was taken, his petition was granted
The hero plunders the dragon's den
The lorn-mooded liegeman. His lord regarded
65
The old-work of earth-folk—'twas the earliest occasion.
When the dragon awoke, the strife was renewed there;
He snuffed 'long the stone then, stout-hearted found he
[78]
The footprint of foeman; too far had he gone
With cunning craftiness close to the head of
70
The fire-spewing dragon. So undoomed he may 'scape from
Anguish and exile with ease who possesseth
The favor of Heaven. The hoard-warden eagerly
Searched o'er the ground then, would meet with the person
That caused him sorrow while in slumber reclining:
75
Gleaming and wild he oft went round the cavern,
All of it outward; not any of earthmen
Was seen in that desert.6 Yet he joyed in the battle,
Rejoiced in the conflict: oft he turned to the barrow,
Sought for the gem-cup;7 this he soon perceived then
The dragon perceives that some one has disturbed his treasure.80
That some man or other had discovered the gold,
The famous folk-treasure. Not fain did the hoard-ward
Wait until evening; then the ward of the barrow
Was angry in spirit, the loathèd one wished to
Pay for the dear-valued drink-cup with fire.
85
Then the day was done as the dragon would have it,
He no longer would wait on the wall, but departed
The dragon is infuriated.
Fire-impelled, flaming. Fearful the start was
To earls in the land, as it early thereafter
To their giver-of-gold was grievously ended.

[1] For 'long-gestréona,' B. suggests 'láengestréona,' and renders, Of fleeting treasures. S. accepts H.'s 'long-gestréona,' but renders, The treasure long in accumulating.

[2] For 'hard-fyrdne' (2246), B. first suggested 'hard-fyndne,' rendering: A heap of treasures ... so great that its equal would be hard to find. The same scholar suggests later 'hord-wynne dæl' = A deal of treasure-joy.

[3] Some read 'fec-word' (2247), and render: Banning words uttered.

[4] An earlier reading of H.'s gave the following meaning to this passage: He is said to inhabit a mound under the earth, where he, etc. The translation in the text is more authentic.

[5] The repetition of 'hord' in this passage has led some scholars to suggest new readings to avoid the second 'hord.' This, however, is not under the main stress, and, it seems to me, might easily be accepted.

[6] The reading of H.-So. is well defended in the notes to that volume. B. emends and renders: Nor was there any man in that desert who rejoiced in conflict, in battle-work. That is, the hoard-ward could not find any one who had disturbed his slumbers, for no warrior was there, t.B.'s emendation would give substantially the same translation.

[7] 'Sinc-fæt' (2301): this word both here and in v. 2232, t.B. renders 'treasure.'

XXXIII.

BRAVE THOUGH AGED.—REMINISCENCES.

The dragon spits fire.

The stranger began then to vomit forth fire,
To burn the great manor; the blaze then glimmered
For anguish to earlmen, not anything living
[79]
Was the hateful air-goer willing to leave there.
5
The war of the worm widely was noticed,
The feud of the foeman afar and anear,
How the enemy injured the earls of the Geatmen,
Harried with hatred: back he hied to the treasure,
To the well-hidden cavern ere the coming of daylight.
10
He had circled with fire the folk of those regions,
With brand and burning; in the barrow he trusted,
In the wall and his war-might: the weening deceived him.

Beowulf hears of the havoc wrought by the dragon.

Then straight was the horror to Beowulf published,
Early forsooth, that his own native homestead,1
15
The best of buildings, was burning and melting,
Gift-seat of Geatmen. 'Twas a grief to the spirit
Of the good-mooded hero, the greatest of sorrows:

He fears that Heaven is punishing him for some crime.

The wise one weened then that wielding his kingdom
'Gainst the ancient commandments, he had bitterly angered
20
The Lord everlasting: with lorn meditations
His bosom welled inward, as was nowise his custom.
The fire-spewing dragon fully had wasted
The fastness of warriors, the water-land outward,
The manor with fire. The folk-ruling hero,
25

Prince of the Weders, was planning to wreak him.
The warmen's defender bade them to make him,
Earlmen's atheling, an excellent war-shield
He orders an iron shield to be made from him, wood is useless.
Wholly of iron: fully he knew then
That wood from the forest was helpless to aid him,
30
Shield against fire. The long-worthy ruler
Must live the last of his limited earth-days,
Of life in the world and the worm along with him,
Though he long had been holding hoard-wealth in plenty.
He determines to fight alone.
Then the ring-prince disdained to seek with a war-band,
35
With army extensive, the air-going ranger;
He felt no fear of the foeman's assaults and
He counted for little the might of the dragon,
[80]
His power and prowess: for previously dared he
Beowulf's early triumphs referred to
A heap of hostility, hazarded dangers,
40
War-thane, when Hrothgar's palace he cleansèd,
Conquering combatant, clutched in the battle
The kinsmen of Grendel, of kindred detested.2
Higelac's death recalled.
'Twas of hand-fights not least where Higelac was slaughtered,
When the king of the Geatmen with clashings of battle,
45
Friend-lord of folks in Frisian dominions,
Offspring of Hrethrel perished through sword-drink,
With battle-swords beaten; thence Beowulf came then
On self-help relying, swam through the waters;
He bare on his arm, lone-going, thirty
50
Outfits of armor, when the ocean he mounted.
The Hetwars by no means had need to be boastful
Of their fighting afoot, who forward to meet him
Carried their war-shields: not many returned from
The brave-mooded battle-knight back to their homesteads.
55
Ecgtheow's bairn o'er the bight-courses swam then,
Lone-goer lorn to his land-folk returning,
Where Hygd to him tendered treasure and kingdom,
Heardred's lack of capacity to rule.

Rings and dominion: her son she not trusted,
To be able to keep the kingdom devised him
60
'Gainst alien races, on the death of King Higelac.
Beowulf's tact and delicacy recalled.
Yet the sad ones succeeded not in persuading the atheling
In any way ever, to act as a suzerain
To Heardred, or promise to govern the kingdom;
Yet with friendly counsel in the folk he sustained him,
65
Gracious, with honor, till he grew to be older,
Reference is here made to a visit which Beowulf receives from Eanmund and
Eadgils, why they come is not known.
Wielded the Weders. Wide-fleeing outlaws,
Ohthere's sons, sought him o'er the waters:
They had stirred a revolt 'gainst the helm of the Scylfings,
The best of the sea-kings, who in Swedish dominions
70
Distributed treasure, distinguished folk-leader.
[81]
'Twas the end of his earth-days; injury fatal3
By swing of the sword he received as a greeting,
Offspring of Higelac; Ongentheow's bairn
Later departed to visit his homestead,
75
When Heardred was dead; let Beowulf rule them,
Govern the Geatmen: good was that folk-king.
[1] 'Hám' (2326), the suggestion of B. is accepted by t.B. and other scholars.
[2] For 'láðan cynnes' (2355), t.B. suggests 'láðan cynne,' apposition to 'mægum.'
From syntactical and other considerations, this is a most excellent emendation.
[3] Gr. read 'on feorme' (2386), rendering: He there at the banquet a fatal wound
received by blows of the sword.
XXXIV.
BEOWULF SEEKS THE DRAGON.—BEOWULF'S REMINISCENCES.

He planned requital for the folk-leader's ruin
In days thereafter, to Eadgils the wretched
Becoming an enemy. Ohthere's son then
Went with a war-troop o'er the wide-stretching currents
5
With warriors and weapons: with woe-journeys cold he
After avenged him, the king's life he took.
Beowulf has been preserved through many perils.
So he came off uninjured from all of his battles,
Perilous fights, offspring of Ecgtheow,

From his deeds of daring, till that day most momentous
10
When he fate-driven fared to fight with the dragon.
With eleven comrades, he seeks the dragon.
With eleven companions the prince of the Geatmen
Went lowering with fury to look at the fire-drake:
Inquiring he'd found how the feud had arisen,
Hate to his heroes; the highly-famed gem-vessel
15
Was brought to his keeping through the hand of th' informer.
A guide leads the way, but
That in the throng was thirteenth of heroes,
That caused the beginning of conflict so bitter,
Captive and wretched, must sad-mooded thenceward
very reluctantly.
Point out the place: he passed then unwillingly
20
To the spot where he knew of the notable cavern,
The cave under earth, not far from the ocean,
The anger of eddies, which inward was full of
Jewels and wires: a warden uncanny,
[82]
Warrior weaponed, wardered the treasure,
25
Old under earth; no easy possession
For any of earth-folk access to get to.
Then the battle-brave atheling sat on the naze-edge,
While the gold-friend of Geatmen gracious saluted
His fireside-companions: woe was his spirit,
30
Death-boding, wav'ring; Weird very near him,
Who must seize the old hero, his soul-treasure look for,
Dragging aloof his life from his body:
Not flesh-hidden long was the folk-leader's spirit.
Beowulf spake, Ecgtheow's son:
Beowulf's retrospect.35
"I survived in my youth-days many a conflict,
Hours of onset: that all I remember.
I was seven-winters old when the jewel-prince took me,
High-lord of heroes, at the hands of my father,
Hrethel the hero-king had me in keeping,
Hrethel took me when I was seven.40
Gave me treasure and feasting, our kinship remembered;
Not ever was I any less dear to him
He treated me as a son.

Knight in the boroughs, than the bairns of his household,
Herebald and Hæthcyn and Higelac mine.
To the eldest unjustly by acts of a kinsman
45
Was murder-bed strewn, since him Hæthcyn from horn-bow
One of the brothers accidentally kills another.
His sheltering chieftain shot with an arrow,
Erred in his aim and injured his kinsman,
One brother the other, with blood-sprinkled spear:
No fee could compound for such a calamity.
'Twas a feeless fight, finished in malice,
50
Sad to his spirit; the folk-prince however
Had to part from existence with vengeance untaken.
[A parallel case is supposed.]
So to hoar-headed hero 'tis heavily crushing l
[83]
To live to see his son as he rideth
Young on the gallows: then measures he chanteth,
55
A song of sorrow, when his son is hanging
For the raven's delight, and aged and hoary
He is unable to offer any assistance.
Every morning his offspring's departure
Is constant recalled: he cares not to wait for
60
The birth of an heir in his borough-enclosures,
Since that one through death-pain the deeds hath experienced.
He heart-grieved beholds in the house of his son the
Wine-building wasted, the wind-lodging places
Reaved of their roaring; the riders are sleeping,
65
The knights in the grave; there's no sound of the harp-wood,
Joy in the yards, as of yore were familiar.
[1] 'Gomelum ceorle' (2445).—H. takes these words as referring to Hrethel; but
the translator here departs from his editor by understanding the poet to refer to a
hypothetical old man, introduced as an illustration of a father's sorrow.
Hrethrel had certainly never seen a son of his ride on the gallows to feed the
crows.
The passage beginning 'swá bið géomorlic' seems to be an effort to reach a full
simile, 'as ... so.' 'As it is mournful for an old man, etc. ... so the defence of the
Weders (2463) bore heart-sorrow, etc.' The verses 2451 to 2463½ would be
parenthetical, the poet's feelings being so strong as to interrupt the simile. The
punctuation of the fourth edition would be better—a comma after 'galgan' (2447).
The translation may be indicated as follows: (Just) as it is sad for an old man to

126

see his son ride young on the gallows when he himself is uttering mournful measures, a sorrowful song, while his son hangs for a comfort to the raven, and he, old and infirm, cannot render him any kelp—(he is constantly reminded, etc., 2451-2463)—so the defence of the Weders, etc.

XXXV.

REMINISCENCES (continued).—BEOWULF'S LAST BATTLE.

"He seeks then his chamber, singeth a woe-song
One for the other; all too extensive
Seemed homesteads and plains. So the helm of the Weders
Hrethel grieves for Herebald.
Mindful of Herebald heart-sorrow carried,
5
Stirred with emotion, nowise was able
To wreak his ruin on the ruthless destroyer:
He was unable to follow the warrior with hatred,
With deeds that were direful, though dear he not held him.
[84]
Then pressed by the pang this pain occasioned him,
10
He gave up glee, God-light elected;
He left to his sons, as the man that is rich does,
His land and fortress, when from life he departed.
Strife between Swedes and Geats.
Then was crime and hostility 'twixt Swedes and Geatmen,
O'er wide-stretching water warring was mutual,
15
Burdensome hatred, when Hrethel had perished,
And Ongentheow's offspring were active and valiant,
Wished not to hold to peace oversea, but
Round Hreosna-beorh often accomplished
Cruelest massacre. This my kinsman avengèd,
20
The feud and fury, as 'tis found on inquiry,
Though one of them paid it with forfeit of life-joys,
Hæthcyn's fall at Ravenswood.
With price that was hard: the struggle became then
Fatal to Hæthcyn, lord of the Geatmen.
Then I heard that at morning one brother the other
25
With edges of irons egged on to murder,
Where Ongentheow maketh onset on Eofor:
The helmet crashed, the hoary-haired Scylfing
Sword-smitten fell, his hand then remembered
Feud-hate sufficient, refused not the death-blow.

I requited him for the jewels he gave me.30
The gems that he gave me, with jewel-bright sword I
'Quited in contest, as occasion was offered:
Land he allowed me, life-joy at homestead,
Manor to live on. Little he needed
From Gepids or Danes or in Sweden to look for
35
Trooper less true, with treasure to buy him;
'Mong foot-soldiers ever in front I would hie me,
Alone in the vanguard, and evermore gladly
Warfare shall wage, while this weapon endureth
That late and early often did serve me
Beowulf refers to his having slain Dæghrefn.40
When I proved before heroes the slayer of Dæghrefn,
Knight of the Hugmen: he by no means was suffered
To the king of the Frisians to carry the jewels,
The breast-decoration; but the banner-possessor
Bowed in the battle, brave-mooded atheling.
[85]45
No weapon was slayer, but war-grapple broke then
The surge of his spirit, his body destroying.
Now shall weapon's edge make war for the treasure,
And hand and firm-sword." Beowulf spake then,
Boast-words uttered—the latest occasion:
He boasts of his youthful prowess, and declares himself still fearless.50
"I braved in my youth-days battles unnumbered;
Still am I willing the struggle to look for,
Fame-deeds perform, folk-warden prudent,
If the hateful despoiler forth from his cavern
Seeketh me out!" Each of the heroes,
55
Helm-bearers sturdy, he thereupon greeted
His last salutations.
Belovèd co-liegemen—his last salutation:
"No brand would I bear, no blade for the dragon,
Wist I a way my word-boast to 'complish1
Else with the monster, as with Grendel I did it;
60
But fire in the battle hot I expect there,
Furious flame-burning: so I fixed on my body
Target and war-mail. The ward of the barrow2
I'll not flee from a foot-length, the foeman uncanny.
At the wall 'twill befall us as Fate decreeth,
Let Fate decide between us.65
Each one's Creator. I am eager in spirit,

With the wingèd war-hero to away with all boasting.
Bide on the barrow with burnies protected,
Wait ye here till the battle is over.
Earls in armor, which of us two may better
Bear his disaster, when the battle is over.
70
'Tis no matter of yours, and man cannot do it,
But me and me only, to measure his strength with
The monster of malice, might-deeds to 'complish.
I with prowess shall gain the gold, or the battle,
[86]
Direful death-woe will drag off your ruler!"
75
The mighty champion rose by his shield then,
Brave under helmet, in battle-mail went he
'Neath steep-rising stone-cliffs, the strength he relied on
Of one man alone: no work for a coward.
Then he saw by the wall who a great many battles
80
Had lived through, most worthy, when foot-troops collided,
The place of strife is described.
Stone-arches standing, stout-hearted champion,
Saw a brook from the barrow bubbling out thenceward:
The flood of the fountain was fuming with war-flame:
Not nigh to the hoard, for season the briefest
85
Could he brave, without burning, the abyss that was yawning,
The drake was so fiery. The prince of the Weders
Caused then that words came from his bosom,
So fierce was his fury; the firm-hearted shouted:
His battle-clear voice came in resounding
90
'Neath the gray-colored stone. Stirred was his hatred,
Beowulf calls out under the stone arches.
The hoard-ward distinguished the speech of a man;
Time was no longer to look out for friendship.
The breath of the monster issued forth first,
Vapory war-sweat, out of the stone-cave:
The terrible encounter.95
The earth re-echoed. The earl 'neath the barrow
Lifted his shield, lord of the Geatmen,
Tow'rd the terrible stranger: the ring-twisted creature's
Heart was then ready to seek for a struggle.
Beowulf brandishes his sword,
The excellent battle-king first brandished his weapon,

100

The ancient heirloom, of edges unblunted,3

To the death-planners twain was terror from other.

and stands against his shield.

The lord of the troopers intrepidly stood then

'Gainst his high-rising shield, when the dragon coiled him

The dragon coils himself.

Quickly together: in corslet he bided.

[87]105

He went then in blazes, bended and striding,

Hasting him forward. His life and body

The targe well protected, for time-period shorter

Than wish demanded for the well-renowned leader,

110

Famous in battle, as Fate had not willed it.

The lord of the Geatmen uplifted his hand then,

Smiting the fire-drake with sword that was precious,

That bright on the bone the blade-edge did weaken,

Bit more feebly than his folk-leader needed,

115

Burdened with bale-griefs. Then the barrow-protector,

The dragon rages

When the sword-blow had fallen, was fierce in his spirit,

Flinging his fires, flamings of battle

Gleamed then afar: the gold-friend of Weders

Beowulf's sword fails him.

Boasted no conquests, his battle-sword failed him

120

Naked in conflict, as by no means it ought to,

Long-trusty weapon. 'Twas no slight undertaking

That Ecgtheow's famous offspring would leave

The drake-cavern's bottom; he must live in some region

Other than this, by the will of the dragon,

125

As each one of earthmen existence must forfeit.

'Twas early thereafter the excellent warriors

The combat is renewed.

Met with each other. Anew and afresh

The hoard-ward took heart (gasps heaved then his bosom):

The great hero is reduced to extremities.

Sorrow he suffered encircled with fire

130

Who the people erst governed. His companions by no means

Were banded about him, bairns of the princes,

His comrades flee!

With valorous spirit, but they sped to the forest,

Seeking for safety. The soul-deeps of one were

Blood is thicker than water.

Ruffled by care: kin-love can never

135

Aught in him waver who well doth consider.

[88]

[1] The clause 2520(2)-2522(1), rendered by 'Wist I … monster,' Gr., followed by S., translates substantially as follows: If I knew how else I might combat the boastful defiance of the monster.—The translation turns upon 'wiðgrípan,' a word not understood.

[2] B. emends and translates: I will not flee the space of a foot from the guard of the barrow, but there shall be to us a fight at the wall, as fate decrees, each one's Creator.

[3] The translation of this passage is based on 'unsláw' (2565), accepted by H.-So., in lieu of the long-standing 'ungléaw.' The former is taken as an adj. limiting 'sweord'; the latter as an adj. c. 'gúð-cyning': The good war-king, rash with edges, brandished his sword, his old relic. The latter gives a more rhetorical Anglo-Saxon (poetical) sentence.

XXXVI.

WIGLAF THE TRUSTY.—BEOWULF IS DESERTED BY FRIENDS AND BY SWORD.

Wiglaf remains true—the ideal Teutonic liegeman.

The son of Weohstan was Wiglaf entitled,

Shield-warrior precious, prince of the Scylfings,

Ælfhere's kinsman: he saw his dear liegelord

Enduring the heat 'neath helmet and visor.

5

Then he minded the holding that erst he had given him,

Wiglaf recalls Beowulf's generosity.

The Wægmunding warriors' wealth-blessèd homestead,

Each of the folk-rights his father had wielded;

He was hot for the battle, his hand seized the target,

The yellow-bark shield, he unsheathed his old weapon,

10

Which was known among earthmen as the relic of Eanmund,

Ohthere's offspring, whom, exiled and friendless,

Weohstan did slay with sword-edge in battle,

And carried his kinsman the clear-shining helmet,

The ring-made burnie, the old giant-weapon

15

That Onela gave him, his boon-fellow's armor,

Ready war-trappings: he the feud did not mention,

Though he'd fatally smitten the son of his brother.

Many a half-year held he the treasures,

The bill and the burnie, till his bairn became able,

20

Like his father before him, fame-deeds to 'complish;

Then he gave him 'mong Geatmen a goodly array of

Weeds for his warfare; he went from life then

Old on his journey. 'Twas the earliest time then

This is Wiglaf's first battle as liegeman of Beowulf.

That the youthful champion might charge in the battle

25

Aiding his liegelord; his spirit was dauntless.

Nor did kinsman's bequest quail at the battle:

This the dragon discovered on their coming together.

Wiglaf uttered many a right-saying,

Said to his fellows, sad was his spirit:

Wiglaf appeals to the pride of the cowards.30

"I remember the time when, tasting the mead-cup,

We promised in the hall the lord of us all

[89]

Who gave us these ring-treasures, that this battle-equipment,

Swords and helmets, we'd certainly quite him,

Should need of such aid ever befall him:

How we have forfeited our liegelord's confidence!35

In the war-band he chose us for this journey spontaneously,

Stirred us to glory and gave me these jewels,

Since he held and esteemed us trust-worthy spearmen,

Hardy helm-bearers, though this hero-achievement

Our lord intended alone to accomplish,

40

Ward of his people, for most of achievements,

Doings audacious, he did among earth-folk.

Our lord is in sore need of us.

The day is now come when the ruler of earthmen

Needeth the vigor of valiant heroes:

Let us wend us towards him, the war-prince to succor,

45

While the heat yet rageth, horrible fire-fight.

I would rather die than go home with out my suzerain.

God wot in me, 'tis mickle the liefer

The blaze should embrace my body and eat it

With my treasure-bestower. Meseemeth not proper

To bear our battle-shields back to our country,

50

'Less first we are able to fell and destroy the

Long-hating foeman, to defend the life of

Surely he does not deserve to die alone.

The prince of the Weders. Well do I know 'tisn't

Earned by his exploits, he only of Geatmen

Sorrow should suffer, sink in the battle:

55

Brand and helmet to us both shall be common,

1Shield-cover, burnie." Through the bale-smoke he stalked then,

Went under helmet to the help of his chieftain,

Wiglaf reminds Beowulf of his youthful boasts.

Briefly discoursing: "Beowulf dear,

Perform thou all fully, as thou formerly saidst,

60

In thy youthful years, that while yet thou livedst

[90]

Thou wouldst let thine honor not ever be lessened.

Thy life thou shalt save, mighty in actions,

Atheling undaunted, with all of thy vigor;

The monster advances on them.

I'll give thee assistance." The dragon came raging,

65

Wild-mooded stranger, when these words had been uttered

('Twas the second occasion), seeking his enemies,

Men that were hated, with hot-gleaming fire-waves;

With blaze-billows burned the board to its edges:

The fight-armor failed then to furnish assistance

70

To the youthful spear-hero: but the young-agèd stripling

Quickly advanced 'neath his kinsman's war-target,

Since his own had been ground in the grip of the fire.

Beowulf strikes at the dragon.

Then the warrior-king was careful of glory,

He soundly smote with sword-for-the-battle,

75

That it stood in the head by hatred driven;

Nægling was shivered, the old and iron-made

His sword fails him.

Brand of Beowulf in battle deceived him.

'Twas denied him that edges of irons were able

To help in the battle; the hand was too mighty

80

2Which every weapon, as I heard on inquiry,

Outstruck in its stroke, when to struggle he carried

The wonderful war-sword: it waxed him no better.

The dragon advances on Beowulf again.

Then the people-despoiler—third of his onsets—

Fierce-raging fire-drake, of feud-hate was mindful,

85

Charged on the strong one, when chance was afforded,

Heated and war-grim, seized on his neck

With teeth that were bitter; he bloody did wax with

Soul-gore seething; sword-blood in waves boiled.

[1] The passage 'Brand ... burnie,' is much disputed. In the first place, some eminent critics assume a gap of at least two half-verses.—'Úrum' (2660), being a peculiar form, has been much discussed. 'Byrdu-scrúd' is also a crux. B. suggests 'býwdu-scrúd' = splendid vestments. Nor is 'bám' accepted by all, 'béon' being suggested. Whatever the individual words, the passage must mean, "I intend to share with him my equipments of defence."

[2] B. would render: Which, as I heard, excelled in stroke every sword that he carried to the strife, even the strongest (sword). For 'Þonne' he reads 'Þone,' rel. pr.

[91]

XXXVII.

THE FATAL STRUGGLE.—BEOWULF'S LAST MOMENTS.

Wiglaf defends Beowulf.

Then I heard that at need of the king of the people

The upstanding earlman exhibited prowess,

Vigor and courage, as suited his nature;

1He his head did not guard, but the high-minded liegeman's

5

Hand was consumed, when he succored his kinsman,

So he struck the strife-bringing strange-comer lower,

Earl-thane in armor, that in went the weapon

Gleaming and plated, that 'gan then the fire2

Beowulf draws his knife,

Later to lessen. The liegelord himself then

10

Retained his consciousness, brandished his war-knife,

Battle-sharp, bitter, that he bare on his armor:

and cuts the dragon.

The Weder-lord cut the worm in the middle.

They had felled the enemy (life drove out then3

Puissant prowess), the pair had destroyed him,

15

Land-chiefs related: so a liegeman should prove him,

A thaneman when needed. To the prince 'twas the last of

His era of conquest by his own great achievements,

[92]Beowulf's wound swells and burns.

The latest of world-deeds. The wound then began

Which the earth-dwelling dragon erstwhile had wrought him

20

To burn and to swell. He soon then discovered

That bitterest bale-woe in his bosom was raging,

Poison within. The atheling advanced then,

He sits down exhausted.

That along by the wall, he prudent of spirit

Might sit on a settle; he saw the giant-work,

25

How arches of stone strengthened with pillars

The earth-hall eternal inward supported.

Then the long-worthy liegeman laved with his hand the

Wiglaf bathes his lord's head.

Far-famous chieftain, gory from sword-edge,

Refreshing the face of his friend-lord and ruler,

30

Sated with battle, unbinding his helmet.

Beowulf answered, of his injury spake he,

His wound that was fatal (he was fully aware

He had lived his allotted life-days enjoying

The pleasures of earth; then past was entirely

35

His measure of days, death very near):

Beowulf regrets that he has no son.

"My son I would give now my battle-equipments,

Had any of heirs been after me granted,

Along of my body. This people I governed

Fifty of winters: no king 'mong my neighbors

40

Dared to encounter me with comrades-in-battle,

Try me with terror. The time to me ordered

I bided at home, mine own kept fitly,

Sought me no snares, swore me not many

I can rejoice in a well-spent life.

Oaths in injustice. Joy over all this

45

I'm able to have, though ill with my death-wounds;

Hence the Ruler of Earthmen need not charge me

With the killing of kinsmen, when cometh my life out

Forth from my body. Fare thou with haste now

Bring me the hoard, Wiglaf, that my dying eyes may be refreshed by a sight of it.

To behold the hoard 'neath the hoar-grayish stone,

50

Well-lovèd Wiglaf, now the worm is a-lying,

Sore-wounded sleepeth, disseized of his treasure.

Go thou in haste that treasures of old I,

Gold-wealth may gaze on, together see lying

[93]

The ether-bright jewels, be easier able,

55

Having the heap of hoard-gems, to yield my

Life and the land-folk whom long I have governed."

[1] B. renders: He (W.) did not regard his (the dragon's) head (since Beowulf had struck it without effect), but struck the dragon a little lower down.—One crux is to find out whose head is meant; another is to bring out the antithesis between 'head'

and 'hand.'

[2] 'Þæt þæt fýr' (2702), S. emends to 'þá þæt fýr' = when the fire began to grow less intense afterward. This emendation relieves the passage of a plethora of conjunctive þæt's.

[3] For 'gefyldan' (2707), S. proposes 'gefylde.' The passage would read: He felled the foe (life drove out strength), and they then both had destroyed him, chieftains related. This gives Beowulf the credit of having felled the dragon; then they combine to annihilate him.—For 'ellen' (2707), Kl. suggests 'e(a)llne.'—The reading 'life drove out strength' is very unsatisfactory and very peculiar. I would suggest as follows: Adopt S.'s emendation, remove H.'s parenthesis, read 'ferh-ellen wræc,' and translate: He felled the foe, drove out his life-strength (that is, made him hors de combat), and then they both, etc.

XXXVIII.

WIGLAF PLUNDERS THE DRAGON'S DEN.—BEOWULF'S DEATH.

Wiglaf fulfils his lord's behest.

Then heard I that Wihstan's son very quickly,

These words being uttered, heeded his liegelord

Wounded and war-sick, went in his armor,

His well-woven ring-mail, 'neath the roof of the barrow.

5

Then the trusty retainer treasure-gems many

The dragon's den.

Victorious saw, when the seat he came near to,

Gold-treasure sparkling spread on the bottom,

Wonder on the wall, and the worm-creature's cavern,

The ancient dawn-flier's, vessels a-standing,

10

Cups of the ancients of cleansers bereavèd,

Robbed of their ornaments: there were helmets in numbers,

Old and rust-eaten, arm-bracelets many,

Artfully woven. Wealth can easily,

Gold on the sea-bottom, turn into vanity1

15

Each one of earthmen, arm him who pleaseth!

And he saw there lying an all-golden banner

High o'er the hoard, of hand-wonders greatest,

Linkèd with lacets: a light from it sparkled,

That the floor of the cavern he was able to look on,

The dragon is not there.20

To examine the jewels. Sight of the dragon

[94]

Not any was offered, but edge offcarried him.

Wiglaf bears the hoard away.

Then I heard that the hero the hoard-treasure plundered,

The giant-work ancient reaved in the cavern,

Bare on his bosom the beakers and platters,

25

As himself would fain have it, and took off the standard,

The brightest of beacons;2 the bill had erst injured

(Its edge was of iron), the old-ruler's weapon,

Him who long had watched as ward of the jewels,

Who fire-terror carried hot for the treasure,

30

Rolling in battle, in middlemost darkness,

Till murdered he perished. The messenger hastened,

Not loth to return, hurried by jewels:

Curiosity urged him if, excellent-mooded,

Alive he should find the lord of the Weders

35

Mortally wounded, at the place where he left him.

'Mid the jewels he found then the famous old chieftain,

His liegelord belovèd, at his life's-end gory:

He thereupon 'gan to lave him with water,

Till the point of his word piercèd his breast-hoard.

40

Beowulf spake (the gold-gems he noticed),

Beowulf is rejoiced to see the jewels.

The old one in sorrow: "For the jewels I look on

Thanks do I utter for all to the Ruler,

Wielder of Worship, with words of devotion,

The Lord everlasting, that He let me such treasures

45

Gain for my people ere death overtook me.

Since I've bartered the agèd life to me granted

For treasure of jewels, attend ye henceforward

He desires to be held in memory by his people.

The wants of the war-thanes; I can wait here no longer.

The battle-famed bid ye to build them a grave-hill,

50

Bright when I'm burned, at the brim-current's limit;

As a memory-mark to the men I have governed,

Aloft it shall tower on Whale's-Ness uprising,

That earls of the ocean hereafter may call it

Beowulf's barrow, those who barks ever-dashing

55

From a distance shall drive o'er the darkness of waters."

The hero's last gift

The bold-mooded troop-lord took from his neck then

The ring that was golden, gave to his liegeman,

The youthful war-hero, his gold-flashing helmet,

His collar and war-mail, bade him well to enjoy them:

and last words.60

"Thou art latest left of the line of our kindred,

Of Wægmunding people: Weird hath offcarried

All of my kinsmen to the Creator's glory,

Earls in their vigor: I shall after them fare."

'Twas the aged liegelord's last-spoken word in

65

His musings of spirit, ere he mounted the fire,

The battle-waves burning: from his bosom departed

His soul to seek the sainted ones' glory.

[1] The word 'oferhígian' (2767) being vague and little understood, two quite distinct translations of this passage have arisen. One takes 'oferhígian' as meaning 'to exceed,' and, inserting 'hord' after 'gehwone,' renders: The treasure may easily, the gold in the ground, exceed in value every hoard of man, hide it who will. The other takes 'oferhígian' as meaning 'to render arrogant,' and, giving the sentence a moralizing tone, renders substantially as in the body of this work. (Cf. 28 13 et seq.)

[2] The passage beginning here is very much disputed. 'The bill of the old lord' is

by some regarded as Beowulf's sword; by others, as that of the ancient possessor of the hoard. 'Ær gescód' (2778), translated in this work as verb and adverb, is by some regarded as a compound participial adj. = sheathed in brass.

XXXIX.

THE DEAD FOES.—WIGLAF'S BITTER TAUNTS.

Wiglaf is sorely grieved to see his lord look so un-warlike.

It had wofully chanced then the youthful retainer

To behold on earth the most ardent-belovèd

At his life-days' limit, lying there helpless.

The slayer too lay there, of life all bereavèd,

5

Horrible earth-drake, harassed with sorrow:

The dragon has plundered his last hoard.

The round-twisted monster was permitted no longer

To govern the ring-hoards, but edges of war-swords

Mightily seized him, battle-sharp, sturdy

Leavings of hammers, that still from his wounds

10

The flier-from-farland fell to the earth

Hard by his hoard-house, hopped he at midnight

Not e'er through the air, nor exulting in jewels

Suffered them to see him: but he sank then to earthward

Through the hero-chief's handwork. I heard sure it throve then

[96]Few warriors dared to face the monster.15

But few in the land of liegemen of valor,

Though of every achievement bold he had proved him,

144

To run 'gainst the breath of the venomous scather,

Or the hall of the treasure to trouble with hand-blows,

If he watching had found the ward of the hoard-hall

20

On the barrow abiding. Beowulf's part of

The treasure of jewels was paid for with death;

Each of the twain had attained to the end of

Life so unlasting. Not long was the time till

The cowardly thanes come out of the thicket.

The tardy-at-battle returned from the thicket,

25

The timid truce-breakers ten all together,

Who durst not before play with the lances

In the prince of the people's pressing emergency;

They are ashamed of their desertion.

But blushing with shame, with shields they betook them,

With arms and armor where the old one was lying:

30

They gazed upon Wiglaf. He was sitting exhausted,

Foot-going fighter, not far from the shoulders

Of the lord of the people, would rouse him with water;

No whit did it help him; though he hoped for it keenly,

He was able on earth not at all in the leader

35

Life to retain, and nowise to alter

The will of the Wielder; the World-Ruler's power1

Would govern the actions of each one of heroes,

Wiglaf is ready to excoriate them.

As yet He is doing. From the young one forthwith then

Could grim-worded greeting be got for him quickly

40

Whose courage had failed him. Wiglaf discoursed then,

Weohstan his son, sad-mooded hero,

He begins to taunt them.

Looked on the hated: "He who soothness will utter

Can say that the liegelord who gave you the jewels,

The ornament-armor wherein ye are standing,

45

When on ale-bench often he offered to hall-men

Helmet and burnie, the prince to his liegemen,

As best upon earth he was able to find him,—

[97]Surely our lord wasted his armor on poltroons.

That he wildly wasted his war-gear undoubtedly

When battle o'ertook him.2 The troop-king no need had

50

To glory in comrades; yet God permitted him,

He, however, got along without you

Victory-Wielder, with weapon unaided

Himself to avenge, when vigor was needed.

I life-protection but little was able

To give him in battle, and I 'gan, notwithstanding,

With some aid, I could have saved our liegelord55

Helping my kinsman (my strength overtaxing):

He waxed the weaker when with weapon I smote on

My mortal opponent, the fire less strongly

Flamed from his bosom. Too few of protectors

Came round the king at the critical moment.

Gift-giving is over with your people: the ring-lord is dead.60

Now must ornament-taking and weapon-bestowing,

Home-joyance all, cease for your kindred,

Food for the people; each of your warriors

Must needs be bereavèd of rights that he holdeth

In landed possessions, when faraway nobles

65

Shall learn of your leaving your lord so basely,

What is life without honor?

The dastardly deed. Death is more pleasant

To every earlman than infamous life is!"

[1] For 'dædum rædan' (2859) B. suggests 'déað árædan,' and renders: The might (or judgment) of God would determine death for every man, as he still does.

[2] Some critics, H. himself in earlier editions, put the clause, 'When … him' (A.-S. 'þá … beget') with the following sentence; that is, they make it dependent upon 'þorfte' (2875) instead of upon 'forwurpe' (2873).

XL.

THE MESSENGER OF DEATH.

Wiglaf sends the news of Beowulf's death to liegemen near by.

Then he charged that the battle be announced at the hedge

Up o'er the cliff-edge, where the earl-troopers bided

The whole of the morning, mood-wretched sat them,

Bearers of battle-shields, both things expecting,

5

The end of his lifetime and the coming again of

The liegelord belovèd. Little reserved he

Of news that was known, who the ness-cliff did travel,

But he truly discoursed to all that could hear him:

[98]The messenger speaks.

"Now the free-giving friend-lord of the folk of the Weders,

10

The folk-prince of Geatmen, is fast in his death-bed,

By the deeds of the dragon in death-bed abideth;

Along with him lieth his life-taking foeman

Slain with knife-wounds: he was wholly unable

To injure at all the ill-planning monster

Wiglaf sits by our dead lord.15

With bite of his sword-edge. Wiglaf is sitting,

Offspring of Wihstan, up over Beowulf,

Earl o'er another whose end-day hath reached him,

Head-watch holdeth o'er heroes unliving,1

Our lord's death will lead to attacks from our old foes.

For friend and for foeman. The folk now expecteth

20

A season of strife when the death of the folk-king

To Frankmen and Frisians in far-lands is published.

The war-hatred waxed warm 'gainst the Hugmen,

Higelac's death recalled.

When Higelac came with an army of vessels

Faring to Friesland, where the Frankmen in battle

25

Humbled him and bravely with overmight 'complished

That the mail-clad warrior must sink in the battle,

Fell 'mid his folk-troop: no fret-gems presented

The atheling to earlmen; aye was denied us

Merewing's mercy. The men of the Swedelands

30

For truce or for truth trust I but little;

But widely 'twas known that near Ravenswood Ongentheow

Hæthcyn's fall referred to.

Sundered Hæthcyn the Hrethling from life-joys,

When for pride overweening the War-Scylfings first did

Seek the Geatmen with savage intentions.

35

Early did Ohthere's age-laden father,

Old and terrible, give blow in requital,

Killing the sea-king, the queen-mother rescued,

The old one his consort deprived of her gold,

Onela's mother and Ohthere's also,

[99]40

And then followed the feud-nursing foemen till hardly,

Reaved of their ruler, they Ravenswood entered.

Then with vast-numbered forces he assaulted the remnant,

Weary with wounds, woe often promised

The livelong night to the sad-hearted war-troop:

45

Said he at morning would kill them with edges of weapons,

Some on the gallows for glee to the fowls.

Aid came after to the anxious-in-spirit

At dawn of the day, after Higelac's bugle

And trumpet-sound heard they, when the good one proceeded

50

And faring followed the flower of the troopers.

[1] 'Hige-méðum' (2910) is glossed by H. as dat. plu. (= for the dead). S. proposes 'hige-méðe,' nom. sing. limiting Wigláf; i.e. W., mood-weary, holds head-watch o'er friend and foe.—B. suggests taking the word as dat. inst. plu. of an abstract noun in -'u.' The translation would be substantially the same as S.'s.

XLI.

THE MESSENGER'S RETROSPECT.

The messenger continues, and refers to the feuds of Swedes and Geats.

"The blood-stainèd trace of Swedes and Geatmen,

The death-rush of warmen, widely was noticed,

How the folks with each other feud did awaken.

The worthy one went then1 with well-beloved comrades,

5

Old and dejected to go to the fastness,

Ongentheo earl upward then turned him;

Of Higelac's battle he'd heard on inquiry,

The exultant one's prowess, despaired of resistance,

With earls of the ocean to be able to struggle,

10

'Gainst sea-going sailors to save the hoard-treasure,

His wife and his children; he fled after thenceward

Old 'neath the earth-wall. Then was offered pursuance

To the braves of the Swedemen, the banner2 to Higelac.

[100]

They fared then forth o'er the field-of-protection,

15

When the Hrethling heroes hedgeward had thronged them.

Then with edges of irons was Ongentheow driven,

The gray-haired to tarry, that the troop-ruler had to

Suffer the power solely of Eofor:

Wulf wounds Ongentheow.

Wulf then wildly with weapon assaulted him,

20

Wonred his son, that for swinge of the edges

The blood from his body burst out in currents,

Forth 'neath his hair. He feared not however,

Gray-headed Scylfing, but speedily quited

Ongentheow gives a stout blow in return.

The wasting wound-stroke with worse exchange,

25

When the king of the thane-troop thither did turn him:

The wise-mooded son of Wonred was powerless

To give a return-blow to the age-hoary man,

151

But his head-shielding helmet first hewed he to pieces,

That flecked with gore perforce he did totter,

30

Fell to the earth; not fey was he yet then,

But up did he spring though an edge-wound had reached him.

Eofor smites Ongentheow fiercely.

Then Higelac's vassal, valiant and dauntless,

When his brother lay dead, made his broad-bladed weapon,

Giant-sword ancient, defence of the giants,

35

Bound o'er the shield-wall; the folk-prince succumbed then,

Ongentheow is slain.

Shepherd of people, was pierced to the vitals.

There were many attendants who bound up his kinsman,

Carried him quickly when occasion was granted

That the place of the slain they were suffered to manage.

40

This pending, one hero plundered the other,

His armor of iron from Ongentheow ravished,

His hard-sword hilted and helmet together;

Eofor takes the old king's war-gear to Higelac.

The old one's equipments he carried to Higelac.

He the jewels received, and rewards 'mid the troopers

45

Graciously promised, and so did accomplish:

The king of the Weders requited the war-rush,

Hrethel's descendant, when home he repaired him,

Higelac rewards the brothers.

To Eofor and Wulf with wide-lavished treasures,

To each of them granted a hundred of thousands

[101]50

In land and rings wrought out of wire:

His gifts were beyond cavil.

None upon mid-earth needed to twit him3

With the gifts he gave them, when glory they conquered;

To Eofor he also gives his only daughter in marriage.

And to Eofor then gave he his one only daughter,

The honor of home, as an earnest of favor.

55

That's the feud and hatred—as ween I 'twill happen—

The anger of earthmen, that earls of the Swedemen

Will visit on us, when they hear that our leader

Lifeless is lying, he who longtime protected

His hoard and kingdom 'gainst hating assailers,

60

Who on the fall of the heroes defended of yore

The deed-mighty Scyldings,4 did for the troopers

What best did avail them, and further moreover

It is time for us to pay the last marks of respect to our lord.

Hero-deeds 'complished. Now is haste most fitting,

That the lord of liegemen we look upon yonder,

65

And that one carry on journey to death-pyre

Who ring-presents gave us. Not aught of it all

Shall melt with the brave one—there's a mass of bright jewels,

Gold beyond measure, grewsomely purchased

And ending it all ornament-rings too

70

Bought with his life; these fire shall devour,

Flame shall cover, no earlman shall wear

A jewel-memento, nor beautiful virgin

Have on her neck rings to adorn her,

But wretched in spirit bereavèd of gold-gems

75

She shall oft with others be exiled and banished,

Since the leader of liegemen hath laughter forsaken,

[102]

Mirth and merriment. Hence many a war-spear

Cold from the morning shall be clutched in the fingers,

Heaved in the hand, no harp-music's sound shall

80

Waken the warriors, but the wan-coated raven

Fain over fey ones freely shall gabble,

Shall say to the eagle how he sped in the eating,

When, the wolf his companion, he plundered the slain."

So the high-minded hero was rehearsing these stories

85

Loathsome to hear; he lied as to few of

The warriors go sadly to look at Beowulf's lifeless body.

Weirds and of words. All the war-troop arose then,

'Neath the Eagle's Cape sadly betook them,

Weeping and woful, the wonder to look at.

They saw on the sand then soulless a-lying,

90

His slaughter-bed holding, him who rings had given them

In days that were done; then the death-bringing moment

Was come to the good one, that the king very warlike,

Wielder of Weders, with wonder-death perished.

First they beheld there a creature more wondrous,

They also see the dragon.95

The worm on the field, in front of them lying,

The foeman before them: the fire-spewing dragon,

Ghostly and grisly guest in his terrors,

Was scorched in the fire; as he lay there he measured

Fifty of feet; came forth in the night-time5

100

To rejoice in the air, thereafter departing

To visit his den; he in death was then fastened,

He would joy in no other earth-hollowed caverns.

There stood round about him beakers and vessels,

Dishes were lying and dear-valued weapons,

105

With iron-rust eaten, as in earth's mighty bosom

A thousand of winters there they had rested:

The hoard was under a magic spell.

That mighty bequest then with magic was guarded,

Gold of the ancients, that earlman not any

The ring-hall could touch, save Ruling-God only,

[103]110

Sooth-king of Vict'ries gave whom He wished to

God alone could give access to it.

6(He is earth-folk's protector) to open the treasure,

E'en to such among mortals as seemed to Him proper.

[1] For 'góda,' which seems a surprising epithet for a Geat to apply to the "terrible" Ongentheow, B. suggests 'gomela.' The passage would then stand: 'The old one went then,' etc.

[2] For 'segn Higeláce,' K., Th., and B. propose 'segn Higeláces,' meaning: Higelac's banner followed the Swedes (in pursuit).—S. suggests 'sæcc Higeláces,' and renders: Higelac's pursuit.—The H.-So. reading, as translated in our text, means that the banner of the enemy was captured and brought to Higelac as a trophy.

[3] The rendering given in this translation represents the king as being generous beyond the possibility of reproach; but some authorities construe 'him' (2996) as plu., and understand the passage to mean that no one reproached the two brothers with having received more reward than they were entitled to.

[4] The name 'Scyldingas' here (3006) has caused much discussion, and given rise to several theories, the most important of which are as follows: (1) After the downfall of Hrothgar's family, Beowulf was king of the Danes, or Scyldings. (2) For 'Scyldingas' read 'Scylfingas'—that is, after killing Eadgils, the Scylfing prince, Beowulf conquered his land, and held it in subjection. (3) M. considers 3006 a thoughtless repetition of 2053. (Cf. H.-So.)

[5] B. takes 'nihtes' and 'hwílum' (3045) as separate adverbial cases, and renders: Joy in the air had he of yore by night, etc. He thinks that the idea of vanished time ought to be expressed.

[6] The parenthesis is by some emended so as to read: (1) (He (i.e. God) is the hope of men); (2) (he is the hope of heroes). Gr.'s reading has no parenthesis, but says: ... could touch, unless God himself, true king of victories, gave to whom he would to open the treasure, the secret place of enchanters, etc. The last is rejected

on many grounds.

XLII.

WIGLAF'S SAD STORY.—THE HOARD CARRIED OFF.

Then 'twas seen that the journey prospered him little

Who wrongly within had the ornaments hidden1

Down 'neath the wall. The warden erst slaughtered

Some few of the folk-troop: the feud then thereafter

5

Was hotly avengèd. 'Tis a wonder where,2

When the strength-famous trooper has attained to the end of

Life-days allotted, then no longer the man may

Remain with his kinsmen where mead-cups are flowing.

So to Beowulf happened when the ward of the barrow,

10

Assaults, he sought for: himself had no knowledge

How his leaving this life was likely to happen.

So to doomsday, famous folk-leaders down did

Call it with curses—who 'complished it there—

[104]

That that man should be ever of ill-deeds convicted,

15

Confined in foul-places, fastened in hell-bonds,

Punished with plagues, who this place should e'er ravage.3

He cared not for gold: rather the Wielder's

Favor preferred he first to get sight of.4

157

Wiglaf addresses his comrades.

Wiglaf discoursed then, Wihstan his son:

20

"Oft many an earlman on one man's account must

Sorrow endure, as to us it hath happened.

The liegelord belovèd we could little prevail on,

Kingdom's keeper, counsel to follow,

Not to go to the guardian of the gold-hoard, but let him

25

Lie where he long was, live in his dwelling

Till the end of the world. Met we a destiny

Hard to endure: the hoard has been looked at,

Been gained very grimly; too grievous the fate that5

The prince of the people pricked to come thither.

30

I was therein and all of it looked at,

The building's equipments, since access was given me,

Not kindly at all entrance permitted

He tells them of Beowulf's last moments.

Within under earth-wall. Hastily seized I

And held in my hands a huge-weighing burden

35

Of hoard-treasures costly, hither out bare them

To my liegelord belovèd: life was yet in him,

And consciousness also; the old one discoursed then

Much and mournfully, commanded to greet you,

Beowulf's dying request.

Bade that remembering the deeds of your friend-lord

40

Ye build on the fire-hill of corpses a lofty

Burial-barrow, broad and far-famous,

As 'mid world-dwelling warriors he was widely most honored

While he reveled in riches. Let us rouse us and hasten

[105]

Again to see and seek for the treasure,

45

The wonder 'neath wall. The way I will show you,
That close ye may look at ring-gems sufficient
And gold in abundance. Let the bier with promptness
Fully be fashioned, when forth we shall come,
And lift we our lord, then, where long he shall tarry,
50
Well-beloved warrior, 'neath the Wielder's protection."
Wiglaf charges them to build a funeral-pyre.
Then the son of Wihstan bade orders be given,
Mood-valiant man, to many of heroes,
Holders of homesteads, that they hither from far,
6Leaders of liegemen, should look for the good one
55
With wood for his pyre: "The flame shall now swallow
(The wan fire shall wax7) the warriors' leader
Who the rain of the iron often abided,
When, sturdily hurled, the storm of the arrows
Leapt o'er linden-wall, the lance rendered service,
60
Furnished with feathers followed the arrow."
Now the wise-mooded son of Wihstan did summon
The best of the braves from the band of the ruler
He takes seven thanes, and enters the den.
Seven together; 'neath the enemy's roof he
Went with the seven; one of the heroes
65
Who fared at the front, a fire-blazing torch-light

159

Bare in his hand. No lot then decided
Who that hoard should havoc, when hero-earls saw it
Lying in the cavern uncared-for entirely,
Rusting to ruin: they rued then but little
70
That they hastily hence hauled out the treasure,

They push the dragon over the wall.

The dear-valued jewels; the dragon eke pushed they,
The worm o'er the wall, let the wave-currents take him,
[106]
The waters enwind the ward of the treasures.

The hoard is laid on a wain.

There wounden gold on a wain was uploaded,
75
A mass unmeasured, the men-leader off then,
The hero hoary, to Whale's-Ness was carried.

[1] For 'gehýdde,' B. suggests 'gehýðde': the passage would stand as above except the change of 'hidden' (v. 2) to 'plundered.' The reference, however, would be to the thief, not to the dragon.

[2] The passage 'Wundur … búan' (3063-3066), M. took to be a question asking whether it was strange that a man should die when his appointed time had come. —B. sees a corruption, and makes emendations introducing the idea that a brave man should not die from sickness or from old age, but should find death in the performance of some deed of daring.—S. sees an indirect question introduced by 'hwár' and dependent upon 'wundur': A secret is it when the hero is to die, etc.— Why may the two clauses not be parallel, and the whole passage an Old English cry of 'How wonderful is death!'?—S.'s is the best yet offered, if 'wundor' means 'mystery.'

[3] For 'strude' in H.-So., S. suggests 'stride.' This would require 'ravage' (v. 16) to be changed to 'tread.'

[4] 'He cared … sight of' (17, 18), S. emends so as to read as follows: He (Beowulf) had not before seen the favor of the avaricious possessor.

[5] B. renders: That which drew the king thither (i.e. the treasure) was granted us, but in such a way that it overcomes us.

[6] 'Folc-ágende' (3114) B. takes as dat. sing. with 'gódum,' and refers it to Beowulf; that is, Should bring fire-wood to the place where the good folk-ruler lay.

[7] C. proposes to take 'weaxan' = L. 'vescor,' and translate devour. This gives a parallel to 'fretan' above. The parenthesis would be discarded and the passage read: Now shall the fire consume, the wan-flame devour, the prince of warriors, etc.

XLIII.
THE BURNING OF BEOWULF.

Beowulf's pyre.

The folk of the Geatmen got him then ready
A pile on the earth strong for the burning,
Behung with helmets, hero-knights' targets,
And bright-shining burnies, as he begged they should have them;
5
Then wailing war-heroes their world-famous chieftain,
Their liegelord beloved, laid in the middle.
The funeral-flame.
Soldiers began then to make on the barrow
The largest of dead-fires: dark o'er the vapor
The smoke-cloud ascended, the sad-roaring fire,
10
Mingled with weeping (the wind-roar subsided)
Till the building of bone it had broken to pieces,
Hot in the heart. Heavy in spirit
They mood-sad lamented the men-leader's ruin;
And mournful measures the much-grieving widow
15
*   *   *   *   *   *   *
*   *   *   *   *   *   *
*   *   *   *   *   *   *
*   *   *   *   *   *   *
*   *   *   *   *   *   *
20
*   *   *   *   *   *   *
The Weders carry out their lord's last request.
The men of the Weders made accordingly
A hill on the height, high and extensive,
Of sea-going sailors to be seen from a distance,
And the brave one's beacon built where the fire was,
25
In ten-days' space, with a wall surrounded it,
As wisest of world-folk could most worthily plan it.
They placed in the barrow rings and jewels,
[107]Rings and gems are laid in the barrow.
All such ornaments as erst in the treasure
War-mooded men had won in possession:
30
The earnings of earlmen to earth they entrusted,
The gold to the dust, where yet it remaineth
As useless to mortals as in foregoing eras.
'Round the dead-mound rode then the doughty-in-battle,
Bairns of all twelve of the chiefs of the people,
They mourn for their lord, and sing his praises.35
More would they mourn, lament for their ruler,

161

Speak in measure, mention him with pleasure,
Weighed his worth, and his warlike achievements
Mightily commended, as 'tis meet one praise his
Liegelord in words and love him in spirit,
40
When forth from his body he fares to destruction.
So lamented mourning the men of the Geats,
Fond-loving vassals, the fall of their lord,
An ideal king.
Said he was kindest of kings under heaven,
Gentlest of men, most winning of manner,
45
Friendliest to folk-troops and fondest of honor.

WAIT!

This book comes with an Epic Bundle of

8 FREE Audiobooks

https://gum.co/epic-8-audiobooks-bundle/secret-2016

Made in the USA
Coppell, TX
12 July 2020

30710932R10095